✔ KU-618-308

AS YOU LIKE IT

BY
LORI WILDE

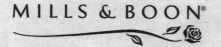

MILLS & BOON®

To Kathryn Lye—
thank you for your sharp eye and great story sense.
Every author should be so lucky to have such an editor.

DID YOU PURCHASE THIS BOOK WITHOUT A COVER?
If you did, you should be aware it is **stolen property** as it was
reported *unsold and destroyed* by a retailer. Neither the author nor
the publisher has received any payment for this book.

*All the characters in this book have no existence outside the
imagination of the author, and have no relation whatsoever to anyone
bearing the same name or names. They are not even distantly inspired
by any individual known or unknown to the author, and all the
incidents are pure invention.*

*All Rights Reserved including the right of reproduction in whole or
in part in any form. This edition is published by arrangement with
Harlequin Enterprises II B.V. The text of this publication or any part
thereof may not be reproduced or transmitted in any form or by any
means, electronic or mechanical, including photocopying, recording,
storage in an information retrieval system, or otherwise, without the
written permission of the publisher.*

*This book is sold subject to the condition that it shall not, by way of
trade or otherwise, be lent, resold, hired out or otherwise circulated
without the prior consent of the publisher in any form of binding or
cover other than that in which it is published and without a similar
condition including this condition being imposed on the subsequent
purchaser.*

*MILLS & BOON and MILLS & BOON with the Rose Device
are registered trademarks of the publisher.*

*First published in Great Britain 2006
by Harlequin Mills & Boon Limited, Eton House,
18-24 Paradise Road,
Richmond, Surrey TW9 1SR*

© Laurie Vanzura 2004

ISBN 0 263 84581 8

14-0106

*Printed and bound in Spain
by Litografia Rosés S.A., Barcelona*

1

"GREAT SEX isn't just about mind-blowing orgasms and Fourth of July fireworks."

Apparently not, Marissa Sturgess thought.

Leaning back in the tweed-cloth swivel chair, she doodled aggressively on her yellow legal pad and listened to Francine Phillips, the lab-coated clinician from the renowned Baxter and Jackson Sex Research Institute, address the Pegasus software team assembled around the paper-strewn wood-laminate conference table. The team consisted of the two remaining account managers—one of whom was Marissa—a system analyst, four programmers and the president of Pegasus, Judd Thompson.

If great sex was just about excellent technique she wouldn't have found a rather insulting Dear Jane letter from her investment-banker boyfriend, Steve, propped against the salt and pepper shakers on her kitchen table that very morning, ending their three-month relationship.

As he put it, she was too intense in life in general and in the bedroom specifically. He needed someone more lighthearted, spontaneous and fun.

Yeah, okay, all right. Obviously, she was so intense

Steve had resorted to dumping her via a scribbled note rather than confronting her face-to-face.

The coward. Running away and robbing her of the opportunity for rebuttal. She'd taken his stupid note, methodically shredded it into a hundred little pieces and flushed it down the toilet.

"Our extensive research with happily married couples has shown us that great sex demands not only trust, caring and honesty, but above all else..." Francine continued and then paused as if waiting for a drumroll.

Marissa tossed her head to shake away all thoughts of Steven J. Thortonberry the Third and get her mind back on the task at hand. She'd already wasted a good ten minutes fretting over the breakup. Enough was enough. Time to move on. She refused to linger on defeat.

Besides, it wasn't losing Steve that bothered her so much as it was his accusation she was too serious in the sack.

"You go at sex like it's a corporate takeover, Marissa. Can't you ever just relax and enjoy the moment?" he'd asked her on several occasions.

In a nutshell? No. To Marissa's way of thinking, relaxation was grossly overrated and a handy excuse for lazy people.

As the only child of Brigadier General Dwight D. Sturgess she had learned to attack life with verve and gusto; giving a hundred and twenty percent to any project she tackled, including sex. Her mother had died when she was a baby and it had just been her and her dad. At an early age, Marissa had discovered being the best was the only sure way to guarantee her father's respect.

Her resulting lust for success had served her well in the business world, but in her personal life...well, in her experience most men didn't appreciate a competitive woman.

At least not when it came to physical intimacy.

And now here was this plump, gray-haired, bespectacled grandmotherly woman standing behind the podium at the head of the conference table, a laser pointer in her hand, lecturing on the fundamentals of great sex. And according to the theory she was putting forth, Marissa simply didn't measure up.

''Truly transcendental sex must include a sense of whimsy.'' Francine used the pointer to highlight her presentation on the plasma screen featuring a laughing woman being pushed on a playground swing by an equally gleeful man.

''Whimsy?'' The other account manager, Dash Peterson, asked.

''Fun, lightheartedness, humor.''

Dash winked suggestively across the table at Marissa. The man was a supreme egotist with a sleazy streak a mile wide. He fancied she wanted him as much as he wanted her and he was her chief competition for the promotion. Unfortunately, while Dash was a royal pain in the keester, he was also damn good at his job.

Marissa ignored him and focused her total attention on Francine. Baxter and Jackson made up thirty percent of Pegasus's entire business and since premature labor had forced the current account director to leave her job three weeks earlier than planned, the sex institute's account was now up for grabs. Whoever ended up managing that piece of the pie stood an excellent chance of becoming the next director.

And Marissa wanted the position more than she wanted to breathe.

For three years she'd been gunning for the job ever since she'd made the switch from systems liaison to marketing and joined the small but up-and-coming Manhattan software company with a very promising future. To that end, she'd done everything in her power to cultivate the right image.

Her goal?

Ooze success and convince everyone around her that she was a winner. If she looked and acted the part, sooner or later she was bound to get what she wanted.

Marissa kept her blond hair cut in a sleek, easy-to-manage, chin-length bob. She spent an hour a day at the gym to maintain the size eight figure she'd had since high school. She knew she wasn't a ravishing beauty with her too-small eyes and her too-wide forehead but she had good cheekbones and she pampered her complexion with a plethora of beauty creams and potions.

And even though it required running up her credit cards a bit, she wore exquisitely tailored suits and look-at-me leather stilettos. Clothes might make the man, but in Marissa's estimation the right footwear—

from Manolo Blahnik to Jimmy Choo to Dolce and Gabbana—made the woman. Not that she was a true shoe-aholic in the vein of some women. It wasn't the shoes themselves that set Marissa's heart aflutter, but rather what those high-fashion accessories whispered to her.

See, Daddy, I am a winner.

So far, her attention to detail had paid off. Her last year's productivity bonus equaled a fourth of her yearly salary. But her success only whet her appetite for bigger and better things. If she got the promotion and made a huge splash as Pegasus's account director, she would enhance her cache with larger software firms. Marissa was determined to eventually become the most respected software-marketing director on the East Coast.

"Could you please elaborate about this whole whimsy thing, Francine? I want to make absolutely sure I have a handle on your proposed project." Dash grinned at the Baxter and Jackson clinician, putting all four of his cheeky dimples into the smile.

Suck-up. Marissa flashed him the message with her eyes.

Don't you know it, he flashed back.

"Why, certainly, Dash. Our extensive two-year study group has shown that a sense of fun is the key to long-term monogamous sex. And you would be surprised at how many couples don't recognize their inner need for spontaneous, impulsive sex play."

What a load of malarkey, Marissa thought. Playing pinch and tickle in the bedroom no more kept a marriage together than holiday traditions. What made a marriage succeed was hard work and dedication and facing problems head-on.

In her personal opinion the Baxter and Jackson research project oversimplified relationships, but hey, they were the clients. She wasn't paid to have a personal opinion. She'd buy into anything they wanted her to buy into.

"Very informative," Dash said. "And your theory explains why Marissa has trouble holding on to a man. She wouldn't know fun if it bit her on the butt."

"I don't..." Marissa almost rose to the bait but then quickly clamped down on her tongue.

If Steve hadn't just walked out on her, Dash's comment wouldn't have rankled. Normally his digs rolled right off her back, but today she yearned to wrap her hands around his neck and throttle him merely for the enjoyment of watching his eyes pop out.

From the opposite end of the conference table Judd Thompson cleared his throat. Judd was in his midfifties, although he looked ten years younger. He had once worked for the largest, most successful software company on the planet, and was the most computer-savvy man Marissa had ever met.

Judd expected a lot from his employees, but he wasn't as demanding as her father. Naturally, he had a more civilian approach to life than the General, but like her old man, he prized achievement. She eagerly turned herself inside out to engender his accolades.

When Judd was happy with her performance, Marissa was happy.

"Pipe down, you two," Judd chided with a frown. "Could we put the petty one-upmanship aside for at least a few minutes and allow Francine to finish detailing her requirements?"

Marissa nodded, sat up straighter and purposefully avoided looking at Dash.

"Thank you, Judd," Francine said. "What we want from Pegasus on this project is a bit different from the software you've created for us in the past."

"How so?" Dash asked.

"We're interested in producing a virtual-reality video game promoting sex play among couples who've found their love life stagnating. An aid, if you will, for our patients who have difficulty letting their hair down and having fun."

"But we don't design video games," piped up one of the programmers. "Especially virtual reality. That requires a completely different set of skills."

"I'm sure we can find a way around that small obstacle," Marissa said, knowing full well the obstacles were anything but small. "I'm prepared to do whatever it takes to keep Baxter and Jackson satisfied."

Take that, Dash.

"I know a freelance designer," Dash interrupted. "I'm sure if you selected me to manage your account I could wrangle a very good deal for you."

"Actually." Francine smiled. "We already have a designer in mind."

"Oh?" Dash looked taken aback.

Marissa very professionally resisted the urge to pitch him a gloating smirk.

"Beau Thibbedeaux," Francine said. "I'm assuming you're all familiar with his work."

A hushed, reverential silence fell over the room. Everyone in the software industry had heard of Beau Thibbedeaux. He was, arguably, the best video-game design architect ever to code a script.

Or at least he used to be.

Dash, Judd, the system liaison and the four programmers exchanged a look. Marissa didn't know the whole story of the Beau Thibbedeaux scandal but apparently it had been a doozy.

The guy had been the biggest star at the largest video-game design company in the country. Hailed as a creative genius, he was a visionary far ahead of his time. From what she could gather through the industry grapevine, Thibbedeaux hated being rushed or pressured.

The rumor was he'd run afoul of a very influential, very impatient overseas client. Beau had simply walked away from the project with an unfinished design left on the table.

Marissa figured Thibbedeaux must have suffered some kind of mental or emotional meltdown because she could not fathom any other reason why the man would hightail it back home to Louisiana and leave the company stranded. Personally, she would rather lie down and die than disappoint her employer no matter how difficult the project or the client.

"Beau's no longer in the business," Judd said, but

Marissa could tell from the speculative expression in his eyes that he would love to be responsible for luring Thibbedeaux back to Manhattan.

"I heard he's a complete recluse," another programmer added.

"The guy retired over two years ago," Dash supplied. "Last I heard he owned a B and B or a restaurant or a bar or something like that in New Orleans."

"We were hoping Pegasus could coax him out of retirement." Francine steepled her fingers and glanced around the table.

"There are plenty of other qualified designers available," Judd said. "Jack Firestein. Ashleigh Henning. Blair Downey to name a few."

Francine was already shaking her head. "But none of those other candidates have Beau's flare for pure, unadulterated fun. We've reviewed his video games. He's the one we want."

"I once worked with Beau. The guy is completely unstable and when he decides to dig his heels in, he digs his heels in. There's no way he's coming back." Dash shook his head.

Dash's easy capitulation surprised Marissa. She'd never known him to give up without a fight. She studied him, trying to figure out his angle.

"I'm sorry to hear you say that." Francine's face reflected her disappointment. "If Pegasus can't make this happen for us perhaps there's another software developer who can."

Oooh, the plot thickens. Why was Francine so insistent on Thibbedeaux?

"Now, Francine, be reasonable," Judd said, attempting to placate her. "If the man is retired, the man is retired."

"We want Thibbedeaux." Francine crossed her arms. For whatever reason, she wasn't going to give an inch on this one.

Judd met Marissa's gaze. She knew that look.

Are you my ace in the hole? Her boss's expression quizzed. He hadn't asked the nonverbal question of Dash, but of her. He'd chosen her as his go-to person. Pride swelled her chest. Yes, yes.

This is your chance. Jump in. Say something. Do it, do it, do it.

Excitement pushed Marissa to her feet. Anticipation had her slapping her palms against the smooth coolness of the tabletop. Enthusiasm had her vigorously nodding her head.

"I can make it happen," she said, the words spilling from her mouth before she'd fully thought this commitment through.

All she knew was a very important client wanted something and it was her job to fill her clients' needs. If she gave Baxter and Jackson what they wanted, Judd would be pleased. And if Judd was pleased, he would give her the promotion.

And the General would stop asking her why she was disappointing him by wasting her time at Pegasus when he felt she obviously would not get promoted there.

The new job would mollify her father. At least for a little while anyway.

Francine beamed at her. "Now that's the kind of can-do spirit I'm looking for."

Marissa possessed the upper hand and she knew it. Francine wanted Thibbedeaux.

Badly.

"We're going to need more money," she dared and thrilled to her own audacity. "This work is beyond the realm of what we normally perform for Baxter and Jackson. We will require twenty-five percent more than our usual fee."

"Fifteen," Francine countered.

"Twenty," Marissa haggled, leaning forward in an aggressive stance. "And you pick up the tab for my travel expenses."

From the corner of her eye she saw Judd watching their interaction like a spectator at Wimbledon, a wide grin on his craggy face. His approval fed her momentum and her boldness.

"Can you assure me you will get Thibbedeaux?" Francine asked.

"You have my word, one hundred percent."

Judd got to his feet. "Could you excuse us for a minute?"

"Certainly," Francine said and wagged a finger. "But I am counting on Marissa to accomplish what she has promised."

How many times had similar words spurred her to climb higher and push harder? Nothing motivated her more than someone's lofty expectations.

Once the door snapped closed with Francine on the other side of it, Dash let out a hoot of laughter.

"What's so funny?" Marissa glared and sank her hands on her hips.

"Boy, are you screwed."

"Just shut up."

"I can't get over the image of you traipsing through the muck of the Louisiana bayou in your la-di-da Manolo Blahniks and your smart little black miniskirt trying to convince a man more hardheaded than a pit bull to return to the city he hates. Priceless."

"Overdoing the melodrama a bit, aren't you, Peterson?" Marissa rearranged her papers. Dash was just jealous because she'd beaten him to the punch.

"And remember, you've got to talk Thibbedeaux into designing a sex video game." He laughed again. "I know Beau. It ain't gonna happen, Sturgess. When you come back with your tail between your legs, a complete failure, I'll be the new account director and you'll be answering to me." He jerked a thumb at his chest.

Dash knew just how to bother her, but if he meant to dampen her resolve with his derision, he'd sorely miscalculated.

"You're just pissy because I had the cajones to commit to the project before you did."

Judd gave a sharp bark of laughter. "She's got you there, Peterson."

"No, I'm just trying to save her from humiliating herself. I know Thibbedeaux and she doesn't. But hey, if she likes having egg plastered all over her face, let her go for it.'' Dash dusted his palms together in a dismissive gesture.

Marissa met Judd's gaze. ''Am I officially managing the Baxter and Jackson account?''

''You did a splendid job of negotiating, Marissa. I'm proud of you,'' her boss said.

She soaked up his praise. She was a sponge expanding to full size. Her chest tightened and her heart floated. But Judd wasn't finished.

''However, Dash is right. Getting Thibbedeaux on board isn't going to be easy.'' He furrowed his forehead. ''The man's a complete eccentric.''

''You don't think I can handle him?''

''It's not you I'm concerned about.''

''I'm not without my charms, Judd.'' She batted her eyelashes.

''Your sex appeal isn't in question here, it's Thibbedeaux. He's a wild card. Are you certain you really want to tackle this obligation? It's better to back out now than not deliver in the end. Don't make a promise you can't keep.''

''If I don't commit to this, we'll lose Baxter and Jackson as clients.''

''Quite possibly.''

''And if I do commit, I greatly improve our bottom line.''

''I take it that means you're going out on the limb,'' Judd said.

Marissa nodded. Challenge was her middle name. The dangling carrot was too juicy to ignore. That and the thought of rubbing the smile off Dash's smug mug.

"I'll guarantee you Thibbedeaux if you guarantee me the account-director position."

"Done," Judd said.

Yes! Mentally, Marissa did a victory dance. She knew just how to celebrate snatching this deal from Dash's teeth.

For the last few weeks an adorable pair of six-hundred-dollar silver-and-azure Jimmy Choo sling backs had been calling her name. With her promotion practically in the bag, she could afford the splurge. After work this evening she was heading straight for Bergdorf Goodman.

Dash waylaid her in the corridor after the meeting. He took her by the elbow and tugged her aside. "Care to make it interesting," he asked.

Marissa eyed him suspiciously. "What do you have in mind?"

"A wager."

"What kind of wager?"

Dash raked a speculative gaze over her body.

"Forget it, you sleaze." She yanked her elbow from his grasp.

"You misunderstand me. Much as I would enjoy the comfort of your hot bod, that's not what I'm proposing."

"No? Then what?"

"Five Benjamins says you can't bring Thibbedeaux in."

Marissa stared at her competitor. The idea that he

was willing to bet against her to the tune of five hundred dollars had doubt creeping around inside her.

''I'm betting you have to sleep with him to get what you want.''

''You are such a jerk-off, you know that? I don't have to lower myself to your level. I can convince Beau Thibbedeaux to take the job without any added sexual enticements.

''A thousand bucks says you can't.'' He extended a hand.

Phooey. She shook off her reservation. She'd proved once and for all she was a better negotiator than Dash.

''It's a deal,'' she said and slapped her palm into his.

2

"WHEN *WAS* THE LAST TIME you got laid?" Remy Thibbedeaux asked his older half brother and silent business partner, Beau.

Remy was polishing the bar with a dish towel and putting out fresh peanuts in anticipation of happy hour. The front door stood open and a light tourist crowd prowled the street. Several weeks from now the entire French Quarter would be wall-to-wall people in town for Mardi Gras.

But this afternoon the small Bourbon Street bar and grill was empty save for the two brothers and Leroy Champlain, a blind jazz musician who napped at the back table, soaking up the sunshine slanting in through the spotless window. His fastidious brother kept the place cleaner than an operating room, which was quite a feat considering their centuries-old location.

Beau sat cocked back on the two rear legs of a cane-bottomed café chair, tugged the brim of his New York Yankees baseball cap down lower over his forehead and took a lazy swig from his beer. "Can't see how that's any of your business."

"I was thinking a pretty female might snap you out of your doldrums."

"Well, you can stop thinking."

"You worry me, Beau. Mopin' around with nothing to do."

"I'm not in the doldrums," he denied. "And I'm certainly not moping."

"So what would you call it?"

"Evaluating my options."

"Bull. You've got nothing to occupy your mind. What with me running the bar and Jenny taking over the B and B you've simply got too much time on your hands."

"Serious evaluating takes time."

"I hope it's your future you're seriously evaluating. It's been over eighteen months since you split the sheets with Angeline."

"I didn't break up with Angeline. She broke up with me."

"'Cause you wouldn't ask her to marry you."

"A man doesn't like to be rushed."

Remy snorted. "You two went together for five years. Can't say as how I blame the woman for wanting a commitment."

"It wasn't commitment that had me dragging my heels and you know it. Angeline and I simply weren't right for each other."

"It took you five years to figure that out?"

"We had our moments."

"She never did get over you leaving Manhattan."

"Nope." Beau took another swig. He had been

nursing the bottle all afternoon and the beer had grown warm. It tasted dry and yeasty. "She didn't understand about connectedness."

Remy shook his head. "You and this connectedness business."

"Try having my childhood and see what you end up yearning for."

"Point taken."

A long companionable silence ensued, punctuated only by the squeak of Remy's towel against the bar's brass railing and Leroy's soft snores.

"Do you ever miss it?" his brother asked a few minutes later.

"Miss what?"

"You know."

"Manhattan?"

"Designing video games."

"I still design them."

"But not for profit. Creating sophisticated computer toys for my kids doesn't count."

"Profit's just another word for selling out."

"Spoken like a true rich man."

"Don't start with me." Beau raised a finger. The one riff that existed between them was the issue of Beau's mother.

Francesca Gregoretti Thibbedeaux MacTavish Girbaldi had been born with a platinum pasta fork in her mouth and a flare for the dramatic. She could trace her family lineage back to Christopher Columbus and she lived life with the full entitlement she believed was her due.

She'd met Beau's dad when she was just sixteen and visiting America on a work visa for a modeling assignment. She'd fallen for Charles Thibbedeaux's charm and he had tumbled for her beauty, not realizing she came from one of the wealthiest families in Europe. When Francesca got pregnant with Beau, Charles had dutifully married her in front of a justice of the peace at city hall and in that one fateful action brought down the wrath of the powerful Gregoretti clan.

And set the stage for the battle zone that became Beau's childhood.

He had been through it all with his mother. Divorce, family squabbles, divorce, the numerous lovers, more divorce. But what hurt him the most were the prolonged periods of estrangement from his father and his two half siblings.

Francesca's little dramas had been played out in lavish backdrops all over the world. A chalet in the Swiss Alps. A villa in Italy. A castle in Scotland. On the Concorde. On a Greek shipping magnate's yacht. Riding the Orient Express.

From the bright lights of Las Vegas to the hustle and bustle of New York City to the exotic crush of Hong Kong, he'd trailed Hurricane Francesca and her wreck of human carnage.

Beau would have given his last breath to have spent his life at his father's treasured ancestral home outside of New Orleans with Jenny and Remy and his sweet-natured stepmother, Camille.

But spoiled, pampered Francesca liked using him as a bargaining tool far too much to ever let him go.

Beau shook his head. He didn't like dwelling on the past.

"You need a purpose in life." Remy slung the white bar towel across his shoulder and plunked down in the chair across from him. "You're adrift."

"I'm waiting."

"For what?"

Beau shrugged. "I'll know it when I see it."

Just then the sound of high heels clicking against concrete and the whiff of honeyed perfume lured Beau's attention to the doorway.

A tall, striking blonde stalked over the threshold and into the bar with the presence of gale-force winds. He certainly knew the type. Had seen such women every day on the streets of New York City, dominating the sidewalks with their intensely focused determination. Tough. Success oriented. Self-centered. He had watched them and pitied them.

They had no connectedness to anything truly meaningful. Everything about them screamed money and status and image.

She looked to be in her midtwenties, maybe a couple of years younger than his own twenty-nine years, with flawlessly applied makeup. She wore an understated but expensive long-sleeved blue silk dress cut in a classic style favored by discerning businesswomen who sought to look professional while maintaining a hint of femininity. Tucked under one arm she carried a slim, black leather briefcase and in the other a small blue clutch purse that matched her outfit.

The only thing about her that was the least bit "out there" were her funky shoes. Fashionable azure-and-silver stilettos completely inappropriate for strolling the French Quarter, but just perfect for showing off miles of long, gorgeous calves.

Her features were more compelling than beautiful. She wasn't fashion-model anorexic, and he admired that about her body. Nice breasts, not too big, not too small, in perfect proportion to rounded hips emphasizing her tapered waist.

Her hair was bobbed in a sleek, chic cut and he could tell she wore wispy bangs in order to camouflage a wide forehead. Her eyes were a little on the small side but he'd always had a thing for women with deep brown eyes that went all squinchy when they smiled. He realized he wanted to see her eyes crinkle and dance.

And he wanted to touch her.

No, *wanted* was too mild a word for what he was feeling. He ached to touch her. To find out exactly what her skin felt like. How smooth, how soft. Suddenly, his fingers burned raw and needy.

Just looking at her made him think of velvet and midnight and satin sheets and sunrise.

If he kissed her, would she taste like forbidden fantasies and sensual sin?

His entire body responded to his unexpected desire and damn if he didn't feel the beginnings of a hard-on. It was lust at first sight.

Obviously, it *had* been too long since he'd gotten laid.

Remy got up from the table, leaving Beau to observe the newcomer from beneath the brim of his baseball cap, and slipped behind the counter. The woman headed straight for the bar as if she knew unequivocally what she wanted.

She definitely was not a tourist. The lady was on a mission.

Beau cocked his head and waited with interest to see what she would order.

A martini? A Manhattan? A cosmopolitan? Certainly not a beer. Never a beer. Not enough prestige in a simple concoction of barley and hops.

"Bonjour, mademoiselle," Remy greeted her, purposefully injecting a heavy layer of the charming thick French Cajun accent the tourists adored.

Beau envied his brother's accent. Between his world travels and Francesca's insistence he take allocution lessons to eradicate any trace of what she disdainfully called "Louisiana good for nothing drawl," he could not shake the resulting smooth, neutral, urbane tonality from his voice no matter how hard he tried.

"Good afternoon." The woman smiled at Remy.

"What you be wantin', *chère?*"

"Perrier." She undid the clasp of her wallet and pulled out a ten-dollar bill. "And some information."

"Information?" Remy raised a quizzical eyebrow at the same time he twisted the top off the bottle and poured the iced mineral water into a glass. A glugging, fizzy sound filled the silence.

As Beau studied the woman, he realized he might have been a bit too hasty in his initial assessment of her. Underneath the indomitable stride, her squarely set shoulders and those forthright eyes, he sensed a certain vulnerability that all the busy activity and high-powered success could not salve. He saw it in the way she hesitated for just a nanosecond, briefly sinking her top teeth into her bottom lip. Drawing her courage?

Maybe she wasn't quite as self-confident as she'd first appeared, but she did a pretty impressive job of hiding it.

That sweet, slight hint of contradiction did something strange to him.

Bam! His heart rate kicked up a notch and his mouth went irrationally dry.

Resolutely, she tucked a strand of hair behind one ear, slid her fanny onto the nearest bar stool and hooked the heels of her stilettos behind the wooden rungs. "I'm looking for Beau Thibbedeaux. Would you happen to know where I could find him?"

Uh-oh. So she was looking for him. Not a good sign. The old familiar queasiness every time his past caught up with him winnowed through his stomach.

He traced his gaze over her body again, this time determinedly ignoring her lush curves and searching for clues to her occupation. Too finely dressed to be a private investigator. Not obedient enough to be one of Francesca's handmaidens. If it weren't for those sexy shoes he would say she was a lawyer.

She probably *was* a lawyer in spite of the shoe fetish. Two years later and he was still dodging fallout from the Migosaki deal gone awry. Good grief, would it ever end? Couldn't they just let a man be?

Well, Remy had gotten his wish. Beau now had something to occupy his mind.

Remy shot a quick glance over at Beau. *Want me to rat you out or not?*

His preliminary impulse was to shake his head, glide right out the side door and disappear into the crowd. But he knew better. He'd learned the hard way you couldn't run from your problems.

Plus this particular problem had the upside of being intriguingly attractive.

And it *had* been a very long time since he'd gotten laid.

But the dark recesses of his brain warned: You know you're not the kind of guy who can kiss and then sprint.

It was true. He had never been able to treat sex casually the way most men seemed to be able to. Other than Angeline, he'd only had one other sexual partner and she had been his high-school sweetheart.

He blamed his inherent sexual loyalty on his basic need for connection. Having grown up in a fractured home with no real place to call his own, getting yo-yoed from one continent to the other, from one step-family to the next, Beau longed for a steady, stable woman he could make a life with. That's why he'd had such trouble letting go of his relationship with Angeline long after it was evident their basic values clashed.

But he wasn't a kid anymore whose mother was too busy pitching hissy fits to pay him the slightest bit of attention. Wasn't it time he overcame his annoying impulse of equating sex with love?

Not that he was jumping to any conclusions about Miss New York City. But his unexpected sexual desire for her did raise a few issues.

"Beau Thibbedeaux?" the woman repeated to Remy. "I understand he's part owner of this bar. Where might I find him?"

Beau pushed up the brim of his cap with one finger and settled his chair firmly on the ground. "I'm Beau Thibbedeaux."

The woman whirled around to face him. Her eyes widened as if seeing him for the first time. "Oh."

"What do you need?"

She planted an optimistic smile on her face and darn if her eyes didn't scrunch up in the cute little way he'd imagined. In the blink of a second, she hopped off the bar stool and took two long-legged strides across the floor, her hand extended dominate side up, leaving him with no choice but to get to his feet and accept her proffered palm.

Her skin was warm against his. Her smell—clean, sophisticated, enticing—teased his nostrils and made him itch to nuzzle the nape of her neck.

"How do you do, Mr. Thibbedeaux? I'm Marissa Sturgess."

Nice name, he thought, but said, "You may call me Beau."

Silently he tried it out. Marissa. He liked the romantic way her name rolled off his tongue. He imagined whispering it in the dead of darkness and felt his body heat up.

Her smile deepened and simultaneously dug a soft place into the center of his solar plexus. He'd had a lot of practice assessing manipulative smiles and he could have sworn hers was genuine.

"Beau," she said and the sound of his name on her lips was positively testosterone stoking.

Bizarrely enough, her eyes seemed to burn him. Everywhere her gaze landed, his skin sizzled. His nose, his cheeks…his lips.

Involuntarily, he lifted a hand to his mouth.

Weird.

"I'm a huge fan," she said.

Fan? Oh no, was she some kind of computer-geek autograph seeker who'd acquired carpal tunnel syndrome from countless hours of playing his most popular video game, *Star Tazer?*

She indicated his baseball cap with a wave of her hand and he laughed. Oh yeah. The Yankees.

He was still trying to puzzle together who she was and what she was doing here when she said, "I was wondering if I might have a moment of your time."

Now, that sounded like the prelude to a sales pitch. She was a saleswoman not a lawyer. Yes. That would explain the shoes.

But not his sudden disappointment because he'd misjudged her smile.

"I'm just the silent partner," he said, jerking a thumb over his shoulder at Remy. "My brother handles all the purchasing orders."

"I'm not selling anything."

He folded his arms over his chest, his hands tucked under his armpits and his feet planted shoulders' width apart. "No? Isn't everyone selling *something?*"

"Can we talk?"

He waved at the chair across the table. She eased into the seat and he plunked down opposite her. Remy hustled over with her Perrier and a fresh beer for Beau.

"Got yourself a live one," Remy whispered. "Go for it."

Marissa's lips curled in amusement. "I appreciate the compliment."

Remy grinned back, nudged Beau in the shoulder with his elbow, winked and nodded at him.

Beau kicked Remy lightly in the shin. *Knock off the matchmaking.*

Thankfully, a couple of customers strolled in and claimed Remy's attention.

"Ignore my brother. He can't stand it because he's married and I'm not."

She dropped her gaze for a fraction of a second and pressed her lips together before raising her head and meeting his eyes once more. There it was again, the hint she didn't feel quite as competent as she hoped to appear.

"Mr. Thibbedeaux. Beau." She took a sip of Perrier, and then settled her hands in her lap. "Why don't I just cut to the chase? I'm an account manager for Pegasus software in Manhattan."

He said nothing, just watched and waited. He'd heard of Pegasus. It was a small but rapidly expanding company that had built their reputation on cutting-edge technology and a penchant for maverick risk taking.

"Our largest client is Baxter and Jackson."

"The sex institute?" He purposely put an emphasis on the word *sex* to see if he could provoke a blush. No such luck. Her professional persona was firmly in place and she wasn't about to encourage him. But, although her lips didn't turn up at the corners, her eyes did crinkle and he felt as if he'd been awarded a grand prize.

"Yes. The sex institute."

"Must make for a titillating work environment," Beau said, exaggerating the first syllable of titillating. He made sure his voice was low and husky and provocative.

"At times."

Cotton candy wouldn't melt in her mouth; her expression was that dry. He wondered what it would take to wet her up from the inside out.

"So what does all this have to do with me?" he ventured, although he had a pretty good idea where the conversation was headed and he was loath for it to roll there. Maybe he was wrong and she would surprise him, he hoped wistfully.

"Baxter and Jackson have commissioned Pegasus to produce a virtual-reality video game for them."

"A touchy-feely video sex romp? I thought Baxter and Jackson were strictly clinical."

"It's an interactive, instructional type game designed to assist couples who have trouble letting themselves go during intimacy."

"You're kidding."

"I'm not. Baxter and Jackson have done considerable research that shows a sense of whimsy is a key ingredient in happy relationships. Apparently a lot of their patients don't know how to instigate their own bedroom fun. Hence the idea for a video game."

"You don't say."

She kept her voice just above a whisper and leaned in closer. "Just between you and me and the fence post, I think it's a preposterous notion, but they are the clients."

"What's so preposterous about it?"

"You shouldn't have to play a game to get closer to your significant other."

"Personally, I've always been a big fan of whimsy in the bedroom. I like toys and games and role-playing. How about you?"

He was being wicked and he knew it, but he couldn't seem to help himself. He had the strangest urge to ruffle her feathers. Maybe it was because she'd ruffled his without even trying and he could not stop thinking about undressing her and discovering exactly what delicious treats lay beyond her composed exterior.

Now here it was at last. The pink flush staining her cheeks. He suppressed a triumphant grin.

She straightened, pulling away from him. "I suppose your sublime appreciation of wacky boudoir antics is why they asked me to contact you about designing the game for them."

"Boudoir antics?" He laughed and wriggled his eyebrows.

"It's an expression."

"Yeah, if you're seventy-five."

"What would you have me say? Love-shack frolics?" She narrowed her eyes and her nostrils flared. "The mattress tango? The sleeping-bag slide? Tube-steak boogie?"

"I was thinking something a little more down and dirty."

Wooo, he'd pushed her hot button and she was fun to tease. He murmured a phrase that would have spurred his Italian grandmother to scrub his mouth out with Ivory.

She glared in irritation. "Get over yourself."

"Excuse me?"

"Do you have to make a joke of everything?"

He shrugged. "Sorry. It's my nature. Survival mechanism."

She drummed her fingernails on the table. "Can we return to the topic at hand?"

"If you insist. I'd much rather bug you about sex. It's so easy to make you squirm."

Ignoring that last comment, she said, "We're prepared to offer you significant compensation if you sign on to the project''

Beau shook his head. He had to admit, the idea of creating a virtual-reality sex video game was intriguing, especially if he would be working closely with Marissa, who, it seemed, could morph into something of a spitfire when she got charged up. And once upon a time he would have found the Baxter and Jackson concept quite challenging. But not anymore.

''I'm sorry you wasted your time coming down here, Ms. Sturgess, but I'm retired.''

''People come out of retirement all the time.''

''Not me.''

''Perhaps if you slept on it.'' She reached up a hand and fingered her beaded necklace.

''Really, I'm not interested.''

She fished a pen from her briefcase, jotted down a number on a cocktail napkin and passed it across the table. ''Would this help persuade you?''

''Money isn't going to win me over.'' He pushed the napkin back toward her without even glancing at it.

''What will it take then?''

''That chapter of my life is over.''

''Why?'' she challenged.

''What do you mean why?''

''You're a young man. You were once one of the best software designers in the world. Why would you walk away from it?''

She met his stare and Beau realized she honestly couldn't fathom why he had left both his career and

New York City behind. Even though he expected it from her, he felt oddly disappointed. She asked the same damn questions Angeline had asked. He couldn't explain it to her, just as he'd been unable to explain it to Angeline. He knew she simply wouldn't understand. Not a success-oriented, achievement-driven woman like her.

"I'm sure there are plenty of designers in Manhattan that would leap at the chance to create this game for you, Ms. Sturgess."

"Marissa," she said and laid her hand over his.

The physical contact weakened his knees, tightened his stomach and made him glad he wasn't standing. She was pulling out the womanly wiles now and God help him, he was susceptible.

"No can do, Marissa." Best to send her on her way posthaste before he got himself into serious trouble.

"Everyone has their price, Beau," she wheedled. "Come on. Tell me. What's yours?"

That approach was not going to work with him. He found it mildly insulting that she wouldn't accept no for an answer, even at the same time he admired her buoyant tenacity.

"You can't afford me."

"How do you know?"

"Trust me on this, you wouldn't be willing to pay my price."

"How do you know unless you tell me what it is?" she insisted.

"And risk getting my face slapped?" He chuckled. "Not hardly."

She ground her teeth. "Don't tease."

"Who's teasing?"

He held her gaze. He wasn't even sure what he was proposing, or even if he was proposing anything, but the jump of sexual electricity between them was undeniable. Why let the opportunity slip through his fingers? Especially when it was past time he learned how to enjoy good sex for its own sake and not as a prelude to commitment.

She sucked in her breath. "Listen, this project would help lots of sexually dysfunctional people improve their lives. Don't you want to help people?"

"Not particularly."

Her forehead wrinkled in shocked surprise. "What happened to you?"

"Life."

She launched in again, arguing in circles, gesturing with her arms, talking faster and faster until he feared she was going to burn up all the oxygen in the room. Like a swivel-hipped running back, she was relying on her verbal speed and agility and commitment to her position to influence him.

Poor woman.

She had no idea she had selected exactly the wrong track with him. If she had only stuck with the sexual banter he might have been persuaded. But when those around him got excited and tried to force him into going along with them, Beau stubbornly dug into his position. He shook his head.

She kept talking, working first one angle and then

another. The woman would have made a terrific filibuster or a kick-ass auctioneer.

"No," he said calmly, dispassionately, when she stopped to take a breath.

Their gazes clashed. Her brown eyes flashed a challenge as clearly as if she'd drawn an épée from its sheath, readied her stance for a lunging round of thrust and parry and uttered *"En garde."*

"Perhaps I wasn't making myself clear enough. If you were to…"

"I said no."

"I don't take no for an answer."

"Guess you're going to have to this time, because I'm not changing my mind."

"I don't believe this. Offer a man a huge amount of money to do something he loves, something he's the best at and he turns you down. Who does that?"

"I do."

"You're impossible." In disgust, Marissa threw her arms into the air and the back of her rapidly moving hand struck his beer bottle.

Like a ten pin smacked by a twenty-pound bowling ball, the bottle rocketed against the wall and shattered, bathing them both in beer.

The brittle sound of unintentional violence snapped off the high ceiling like whiplash. Every patron in the place turned to rubberneck, and for the first time Beau noticed the bar was more than half-full and Leroy was no longer sitting at the back table.

"Oh, oh," Marissa sputtered, her eyes widening at what her strong-chinned zeal had wrought.

"Wow," Beau drawled then lazily licked beer foam from his lips. His words were light, but his chiding expression was not. "Impressive display of pique."

"I'm sorry," she apologized and took a deep breath. "I didn't mean to lose control."

"If you were trying to intimidate me, it's not going to work."

"I didn't break the bottle on purpose." Beer dripped from her bangs and she looked incongruously, impossibly cute. Sort of like a Tasmanian devil dressed up in fancy clothes.

"Maybe not consciously, but you were frustrated," he pointed out.

"What are you accusing me of?" she demanded.

Remy rushed to the rescue with two towels and a broom. He handed them each a towel, then started sweeping up the glass.

"So," Remy mused aloud as Beau and Marissa, still locked in a stare, wiped themselves off. "This is what happens when an irresistible force meets an immovable object."

3
_____

MARISSA HADN'T EXPECTED the guy to be so good-looking. Or so damn stubborn.

Dash warned you.

To hell with Dash. She wasn't about to let his doom-and-gloom predictions affect her. She was a professional. The best. She didn't give up easily. She had guaranteed Judd and Francine that she could deliver Beau Thibbedeaux and by hook or by crook she was determined to achieve her goal.

After knocking over Beau's beer bottle, she'd left the bar in a fluster, disturbed by her body's intense reaction to the man and unnerved by the fact she had lost her temper. She needed some distance and time to regroup before mentally wrestling with him again.

She just had to find out what made the guy tick. Obviously, it wasn't money. This afternoon she had made a monster mistake in trying, by sheer will of her personality, to convince him to take the job. What she needed was a more subtle approach.

What she needed was an angle.

Ashamed that she hadn't done more extensive research on Beau before showing up in New Orleans, Marissa crawled into bed in her jammies, whipped open her laptop and plugged it into the phone jack behind the nightstand in her hotel room.

Tackling the task with zeal, she logged on to the Internet. She did a Google search, keyboarding in the name Beau Thibbedeaux, and was rewarded when a string of references popped up. She read each entry with interest, searching for his history, his weaknesses, his appetites, anything and everything that might lend her an edge in dealing with the guy.

What she discovered dampened her enthusiasm. He was an eccentric computer genius. He was rich beyond her wildest imaginings. That explained his cavalier attitude toward money. He seemed to enjoy hiding out from the world, preferring to spend his time with a small but close-knit circle of family and friends.

Beau was a homebody and homebodies were harder to motivate. Absentmindedly, she toyed with a paper clip fished from her briefcase and pondered the situation.

Think. You can do this. You must do this, her internal taskmaster, who was the emotional equivalent of a chain-gang guard on Benzedrine, insisted. *Everyone's depending on you to sign him.*

Well, except for Dash, he was counting on her to fail. She suppressed the fear wading around uncomfortably inside her stomach. She had a lot riding on this outcome. She could not afford to stumble. At the image of Dash's smugness over her failure, fresh determination rose within her.

Albeit determination mingled with a tinge of guilt.

Some people might say she was pushing too hard. If Beau wasn't interested she should simply accept the fact and move on. But Marissa wasn't a quitter, never had been, never would be. She wanted the account directorship, and by gum, she intended to do everything within her power to get it.

Fisting her hand around the paper clip, she closed her eyes and replayed the mental tape of her disastrous first encounter with Beau.

In her mind's eyes she could see him, cocked back on the legs of that chair, a slow, mischievous I'm-up-to-no-good grin lighting up his lips the minute she'd marched into the bar. He exuded a sultry masculinity that called to her.

And turned her on.

Sighing, she opened her eyes and restlessly linked a second paper clip to the first.

They'd shared an instant connection. An ephemeral, nonspecific sort of "hey there" feeling one didn't run across every day. She'd certainly never felt anything quite like it, and their unexpected bond still held the power to affect her, even several hours later.

She chained a third paper clip to the first two, then another and another.

Not to mention he was handsome as sin and possessed a muscular body that bespoke hours in the gym. She ran her tongue over her lips just thinking about his full biceps. She admired a man who was dedicated to health and fitness. Then again, what else did the guy have to do but stay in shape?

It wasn't just his body that attracted her. The soulful expression in his eyes called to her, as well. The aura of loneliness clinging to him made her want to cuddle him.

Yes, there had been a spark.

But then she'd gone and spoiled it all by moving too soon and speaking too fast. Now the damage had been done and repairing her mistake was going to be a lot harder than making a good first impression would have been. Why hadn't she been more attuned to the nuances rippling between them?

Why? Because the man rattled her.

To the bone.

And she didn't like being rattled.

Something about the manner in which he'd studied her, as if he knew exactly what she looked like naked, panicked her in a way she couldn't explain.

Even now, recalling how his silver-gray eyes had leisurely tacked their way up and down her body caused Marissa to shiver involuntarily.

Why was she even thinking like this? Steve had just broken up with her. The last thing she wanted was to get involved with a potential coworker, especially since it would greatly complicate things.

Maybe her botched relationship with Steve *was* the reason why. Steve wasn't the first lover to walk on her because she was too single-minded. Marissa hated to fail at anything and in most areas of her life, she was very successful, but when it came to romance, she didn't seem to have what it took to make relationships last beyond a few months.

All the more reason to stop fantasizing about Thibbedeaux.

But what a smile he had! Slow and seductive and charming.

Snap out of it, Marissa Jane. Keep your head in the game.

Their personal styles were diametrically opposed. Where she was proactive, he was reactive. She was industrious and precise and energetic. Beau was laidback and easygoing and languid.

Or at least he had been until she'd pressured him. Clearly, coercion did not work with this dude.

So what did?

She reviewed their conversation again, searching for places when things had gone well.

During their first exchange of smiles and handshakes, she had definitely gotten receptive vibes from him. But once they started talking, everything had gone downhill from there.

Except, Marissa recalled, he'd enjoyed teasing her about sex. Not that she'd been thrilled with his innuendo. She'd felt as if he'd been making fun of her.

Then again, maybe she was too sensitive. After Steve ditching her and Francine's lecture on the importance of whimsy, maybe Beau's insinuation that she didn't know how to have fun had simply struck a raw nerve.

Was there some way she could turn his fondness for fun to her advantage?

Marissa looked down and realized she'd unknowingly created a paper clip necklace, and in that silly bit of office-supply jewelry, she came full circle.

She smacked herself on the forehead with the palm of her hand.

Duh! Of course! That's what she needed.

A link, a chain, a connection.

Why hadn't she recognized it before? He was a Southern man and Southern men generally cared deeply about home and family. They liked to be charmed and cajoled and coaxed. If there was one sure way to win him over to her way of thinking, adopting his idealized view on life stood the best chance of winning out.

It might not be perfectly honest and aboveboard to tap into his basic human needs in order to snare him, but capitalizing on physical attraction certainly wasn't immoral or illegal or even unethical. It was simply a man/woman thing.

Use what you've got. Show a little cleavage, act contrite about what happened at the bar, smile a lot, slant him coy glances from the corner of your eye. Take things slow.

It wasn't the way she normally did business, but mirroring his needs by indulging in flirtation was harmless enough.

Yep. Take advantage of the sexual chemistry. That was the ticket.

Bet you a thousand dollars you can't win the guy over without sleeping with him. Dash's taunt rang in her head.

Well, Dash was wrong. She could and she would

persuade Thibbedeaux without stepping over the line. Yes, she might use her womanly wiles to convince him, but she wouldn't go any further than flirtation.

Act available, be unattainable.

Marissa smiled and began to hum a song about industrious ants knocking over rubber-tree plants. She knew exactly what she was going to do next.

BEAU SAT in a rocking chair on the back porch of Greenbrier Plantation and gazed out at the riverboat cruising down the Mississippi. Anna, the family's seven-year-old golden retriever, lay at his side. After he had made his first million designing video games, he'd bought back the Thibbedeaux ancestral home that his father had been forced to sell in order to pay for his numerous custody battles with Francesca.

Reestablishing old connections. Restoring his links to the past. Making up for what he had missed out on all those years.

He'd refurbished the small but stately manor into a B and B and then turned it over to his half sister, Jenny, to run. She'd done a damn fine job of it and now the place was usually booked solid year round. Except for the attic room Jenny always kept available for Beau's unexpected appearances.

The early-January wind was brisk but not uncomfortable and it tousled a lock of hair over his forehead. He'd left New Orleans yesterday evening after his odd encounter with Marissa Sturgess and made the twenty-mile journey northwest of the city in an attempt to get the vexing woman off his mind.

The powerful sexual attraction he felt for her spooked him. Beau wasn't accustomed to such rampant physical desires, especially toward a woman who provoked all his worst qualities.

He was damn glad she'd given up and gone on back to New York after the beer-bottle incident. If she had kept pestering him, he didn't know if he would have had the courage to resist her. He was that damn attracted. And the last thing he needed was to get involved with a woman who charged through life stuck in high gear.

Been there, tried that.

Marissa never took the time to smell the daisies or stroll through the grass barefoot and feel the dew between her toes. She never just sat on the porch and watched the river roll by. Even if she went to a trendy spa and paid people to rub the physical kinks from her body, she never mentally let go for a moment.

He knew this about her because he used to run the same fast-track lifestyle she was racing and it had almost killed him. Beau knew what she needed, even if Marissa did not. She needed to find the joy in just being alive. She needed to lie on her back on a blanket and look up at the stars. She needed to roller-skate and roast marshmallows around a campfire and catch lightning bugs in a jar.

She needed to let go of her high ideals and lofty expectations. She needed to value herself first and foremost as a human being and not solely for what she could produce. She needed for someone to strap her to a rocking chair and make her sit there until she really saw what was going on around her.

Or maybe she needed someone to tie her to the bed and give her the most mind-altering orgasms of her life.

Beau grinned at the provocative image.

Thank heavens she'd left Louisiana or he just might have volunteered. This sex-simply-for-the-sake-of-good-sex idea would not be such a hard concept to master if it involved someone as enticing but inaccessible as Marissa.

He also hated that he couldn't seem to stop thinking about her job offer. Already his creativity—which had pretty much gone underground after he'd left New York—roared back to life with a startling vengeance. Consumed by a tumble of ideas for the video game, he'd barely slept last night.

"I'm not doing it," he muttered. "I'm not going back. I can't go back."

The thought of returning to the high-pressure world that drained every ounce of fun from him caused Beau to shudder. He might currently be directionless, but it was a damn sight better than feeling as if your life had been stolen and your very soul sucked dry.

Still, tempted a part of him, *it might be a kick to try your hand at designing a sexual video game.*

His grin widened at the idea of playing that very game with Marissa and goose bumps actually broke out on his forearm. He blamed the cool breeze but he knew he was fooling himself. Marissa was what had him feeling tense and restless, not the chilly air.

"Forget that woman. She's nothing but trouble."

Ignoring his direct order, his psyche delivered up a mental picture of her. Intelligent brown eyes, determined chin, forceful carriage, firm caboose and her take-no-prisoners strut.

He got excited all over again.

"Easy, bucko, she's a man-eater."

Anna lifted her head, whined and gazed at Beau expectantly.

"No, not you. Go back to your nap."

The dog thumped her tail but made no move to get up. He reached down and stroked her golden head that uncannily enough was almost the same color as Marissa's hair. How come women couldn't be as loyal and uncomplicated as man's best friend?

Yes, considering the way he was dwelling on her it was a very good thing she'd left town.

He heard tires crunch on the graveled driveway in front of the house and he glanced at his watch. Tenthirty. A little early for guests to be checking in, but the Scarlett O'Hara Room was vacant.

The sound of a car door opening punctuated the quiet followed by the aggressive strains of a hip-hop beat. He furrowed his forehead in surprise. Most of Greenbrier's guests consisted of older couples seeking to avoid the hustle and bustle of New Orleans or history buffs looking to revisit the past. Neither of whom seemed the type to listen to Snoop Doggy Dog.

To each his own. Beau shrugged it off. He'd go help with the luggage.

Anna sprang up the minute he got to his feet, wagging her tail and ready for action. He bent down to retrieve her Frisbee and tossed it out across the lawn before turning and heading around the side of the house.

Snoop Dogg snapped off in midsentence and the car door slammed shut.

Leisurely Beau sauntered around the corner, Anna at his side with her slobbery Frisbee in tow. He saw a fire-engine-red Thunderbird convertible parked beside one of the ancient magnolias lining the driveway.

Flashy wheels, he thought, and wondered just who was driving the car, but the trunk was up, blocking his view of the occupant.

Maybe it was one of Jenny's friends.

Ambling closer, he could make out a woman's shapely backside protruding from the trunk. Beau squinted against the sunlight and discovered she wore a tushy-hugging black miniskirt and four-inch high heels. Peculiar travel outfit.

His curiosity was definitely aroused.

She pulled a suitcase from the trunk, set in on the ground, then straightened and gazed toward the veranda. The direct sunlight slanted through the magnolia leaves, bathing in her silhouette. She turned her head and he caught a glimpse of her exquisite profile.

Something about her looked very familiar.

A sense of wariness stopped him in his tracks. She hadn't spotted him. Shouldering her luggage, she turned and stalked toward the house.

It wasn't! It couldn't be.

But it was.

His heart dropped into his stomach.

There, looking for all the world like General Patton storming his enemies' stronghold marched Marissa Sturgess, stilettos and all.

"WHAT IN THE HELL are you doing here?"

"My goodness, where's your famous southern hospitality?" Marissa put on a calm, cool facade but inside, her knees were quaking and her heart was doing the cha-cha-cha.

Beau Thibbedeaux had scooted up the path in front of her and he was now blocking her way, his hands fisted on his narrow hips. He didn't appear any too happy to see her. In fact, he looked really mad.

"What are you doing here?" Beau repeated with a growl.

"Why, I've taken a room for the night. The Scarlett O'Hara, I believe it's called." She forced a light-hearted tone into her voice.

"I thought you went back to New York."

"I don't know where you got that idea. I never said I was leaving."

"I told you no."

"Can't a girl take a vacation?"

"Not at my sister's B and B."

"Why not? The local guidebook gave it an excellent rating."

"How did you know I was here?" He glared.

Time to drop the pretense. He wasn't going to play the game.

"I went by your house in New Orleans and your

housekeeper told me where to find you,'' Marissa admitted.

''So you just thought you'd come right up here and be a thorn in my side.''

Charm him.

She smiled. ''Something like that.''

''Well, you can just forget about it.''

''Now, now. I came here to beg your forgiveness. My behavior yesterday was inexcusable.''

''You're going to stand there and try to tell me you didn't come here to coax me into taking on your design project?'' he accused.

''Hello,'' called out a pretty young woman from the wide front porch. ''You must be Marissa Sturgess.''

Marissa peered around Beau's shoulder and wriggled her fingers. ''Hi, yes I am and you must be Jenny.''

''Uh-huh, and this is my rude brother who's letting you cart your own suitcase. Beau,'' Jenny chided him, ''please take Ms. Sturgess's things to her room.''

Marissa dropped her suitcase at Beau's feet and blithely walked around him.

She extended her hand to the auburn-haired, freckle-face woman with a winning smile who came down the steps to greet her. Jenny was dressed casually in blue-jeans overalls, a white long-sleeved turtleneck sweater and blue-and-white Keds. She had the kind of friendly, open face that made you want to tell her everything about yourself all at once.

''I would like it if you called me Marissa.''

"Of course, Marissa, welcome to Greenbrier."
Jenny linked her arm through Marissa's. "Let me
show you the house."

They went on ahead, leaving Beau to bring up the
rear with her suitcase.

Jenny began to tell Marissa about the house and its
history, and while she was very interested, she
couldn't get her mind off the fact Beau was glaring
at her so hard her neck was perspiring.

This wasn't working out quite as she had planned.
It was a little hard to flirt with a man who acted as if
her face was on the wanted poster at the post office.
She had no idea she had upset him to this degree the
day before. So much for charm. Apparently he wasn't
one to easily forgive and forget.

Jenny guided her up the sweeping staircase and
past a hallway chock-full of antique rocking chairs.
"My mother is a rocking-chair connoisseur," she explained. "We even hold a rock-off every summer."

"A rock-off?"

"The annual rocking-chair finals. Last year one of
the contestants made it into the *Guinness Book of
World Records* for most consecutive hours spent
rocking."

It sounded like a fate worse than death and Marissa
found all those rockers lined up a little spooky-
looking. They put her in mind of mobile coffins. But
she was concentrating hard on adopting the Southern
lifestyle long enough to win Beau over.

"You've got some beautiful pieces here," she
commented, the scent of Beau's sweet basil–scented

cologne toying with her nostrils. To distract herself from his disconcerting aroma, she stroked the arm of a nearby rocker. It glided smoothly like satin, without a single creak or groan.

How someone under the age of eighty could sit here and rock for hours on end was beyond her. *Guinness Book of World Records* champion or not.

"Are you a collector?" Jenny asked.

"No, not really," Marissa admitted.

"Oh. I thought you might be in town for the antiques auction at the Conroy estate."

"She's here," Beau muttered darkly, "to drive me crazy."

Jenny turned and looked at Beau. "Do you two know each other?"

"We met yesterday," Marissa explained.

"She showed up at the bar trying to get me to go back to Manhattan and design sex video games for her."

"No kidding?" Jenny looked surprised.

"It's not like that." Marissa glared at Beau. The way he said it made her sound like a pervert. "The videos are for Baxter and Jackson. You know, to help the clinic's patients overcome sexual dysfunction. It's completely tasteful."

"Cool." Jenny grinned.

"You like the idea?" Beau blinked at his sister.

"I think it's a great idea."

"Good grief."

"I can see how designing a sex video game might

drive you crazy,'' Jenny teased. ''Seeing as how you haven't been with a—''

''Hush!'' Beau commanded and Jenny shut up.

But not before Marissa caught the gist of what the younger woman was saying. Apparently it had been quite a while since Mr. Thibbedeaux had enjoyed sex with a partner.

Marissa grinned.

''I think you should do it,'' Jenny said to Beau.

''You think I should go back to Manhattan?'' Beau frowned.

''Oh, not that part.'' Jenny waved a hand. ''You were miserable in New York. But couldn't you just design the game from here?''

Marissa snapped her fingers. ''Of course he could. You're a genius.''

The concept had never occurred to her. The level of effort would be easier to keep tabs on him in Manhattan, of course, because that's where the programmers were, but if a long-distance arrangement was the only way she could get him to sign on, then why not? She had already negotiated her travel expenses into the contract, so shuttling back and forth shouldn't bother Judd.

''Beau really needs something to do,'' Jenny said. ''He loves designing video games but he's got this thing against competition. Totally weird.'' She rolled her eyes.

''Back off, the both of you,'' Beau snapped. ''You're discussing this as if it's not my decision to make.''

He stalked past them, opened the door to one of the bedrooms and deposited Marissa's luggage on the floor. Then without another word, he turned and disappeared down the stairs.

Marissa blew out her breath. "That went down like rock salt."

"Oh, he's just blowing off steam. He does it when he's feeling cornered, but if you really want to know, I can tell you how to handle him."

"Spill!" Marissa grabbed Jenny's arm.

"Boy, you are eager to make this happen." Jenny chuckled.

"The promotion I've wanted for three years hinges on me signing him."

"Well, I have to warn you, it takes him a long time to make a decision. Be patient."

"Gotcha."

"He rebels under pressure, nagging or complaining. Goes back to life with his mother."

"You two don't have the same mother?"

"We're half siblings. Francesca is a terror. She's a diva to end all divas." Jenny shook her head. "I barely knew Beau until he was old enough to get away from her. But that's a long-drawn-out story. What you need are the Cliff Notes."

Marissa nodded.

"Do you really want to know the best way to get him to agree to develop the game for you?" Jenny enticed.

"Oh, absolutely." She would do almost anything

to make this deal happen, even if it meant donning kid gloves and an asbestos suit in order to handle Beau Thibbedeaux.

Jenny grinned. ''Then play with him.''

4

WITH ANNA TROTTING at his heels, Beau sauntered toward the two-story detached garage, whistling under his breath, determined to ignore the walnut of agitation lodged low in his belly. That's what fast-paced people excelled at—disturbing the rest of the world with their high-pressure hurry, hurry, hurry, go, go, go tactics, twisting everyone else into knots.

Well, he wasn't going to let her get away with it. So, Marissa had shown up here unexpectedly. He was calm. He was cool. He was unruffled. He would think of a creative, easygoing way to get rid of her.

The tortoise eventually bests the hare.

Grinning at the naughty idea brewing in his brain, he opened the garage door and flicked on the overhead fluorescent lights. He squeezed past Jenny's little red Honda Civic, parked too close to the lawn tractor and the other gardening equipment, and made a beeline for the staircase.

Upstairs in the loft he found what he was looking for. The boyhood treasures his father had bought for him and Francesca would never let him keep at her house.

While Anna sniffed around searching for hidden

treasures, Beau dug through his past, unearthing an electric train set his dad had mounted on plywood. He found a pogo stick. Stilts. A skateboard. Two bikes. A football gone flat. A seasoned baseball glove. Model airplanes. Plastic army soldiers. A box of broken crayons. Board games—Monopoly, Clue, Life, Backgammon, Twister.

In one corner hunkered his drum set. As a kid, whenever he felt perturbed with his life, he would sneak up here to bash away his demons. He sank down on the stool behind the drums and blew a layer of dust off the cymbals. He reached for the drumsticks. The grip had eroded to a smooth groove from years of practice. He drummed a couple of riffs and Anna took off.

Bang, crash, bang.

A familiar serenity stole over him and he felt the tension drain from his shoulders. And as he played, he plotted.

Hmm, what would drive an express-lane kind of woman like Marissa around the bend and over the edge of her emotional cliff?

Anything slow or plodding.

Anything she might deem trivial or frivolous.

Anything that made her stop, take stock and consider why she required constant activity in order to feel fully alive.

What he needed was an idea that incorporated all three elements. Something unhurried and lighthearted and thought-provoking. Something that was bound to send her fleeing home to Manhattan and leave him in peace.

The truth was, he liked his rut. It felt as comfortable as the soft, worn spot on his drum skin that vibrated dully when he rapped against it with the base pedal.

Bang, bang, crash, thump.

He tapped his foot. Thump, thump, thump drummed the base pedal against the soft spot. He liked the distant, hollow sound it created.

How do you solve a problem like Marissa?

How indeed?

Beau could only think of one thing that incorporated all three elements guaranteed to challenge her single-minded, success-oriented work ethic. Only one solution promised to send Marissa scurrying back to the land of power suits and concrete as fast as her gorgeous legs would carry her.

Sweet, leisurely, frolicsome sex.

His breathing quickened and so did the pace of his drumming.

Bang, clash, clash. Bang, bang.

Beau pumped the base pedal, enlivened by the train of his wicked thoughts.

Thump. Thump. Thump. Thump.

All at once he knew what he had to do.

He would tell her that he would take the job if she would agree to stay with him during the time it took to create the software. She would be looking at six weeks or possibly even longer in the bayou.

But what if she took him up on his offer?

Intriguing question. Well then, her acceptance of his conditions would prove exactly how committed she was to her job and just how deeply she was lost and how much she really needed an intervention. If he had to sacrifice himself for her salvation, then so be it.

Instituting his plan was a calculated gamble and he knew it. But even if he failed, what a way to lose. Besides, if things went well, he stood to gain something invaluable out of the deal. Once and for all, he would discover the secret of learning how to separate sex and love.

Thump, thump, thump…*whoomp.*

Each riff, Beau felt, led him closer to something monumental. He was acutely aware all at once of a shift, of flux, of opportunity.

The base pedal contacted hard and plowed straight through the fragile old drum skin. The weak spot had fractured.

What had once been a small comfortable groove in the diaphanous barrier was now a torn and gaping hole.

MARISSA AND JENNY sat in the cozy kitchen of the B and B sipping espresso and eating delicious home-made banana-nut bread slathered with butter. Sinfully fattening and Marissa enjoyed every bite without even once wondering how long she would need to run on the treadmill to burn off the calories.

The family's big fluffy golden retriever had settled at Marissa's feet and whenever she looked her way, the dog would thump her tail. She was surprised that Anna had taken a liking to her. She had never had a pet, didn't know how to act around them. As a kid, the General had forbidden them as sentimental time wasters. As an adult, she simply had been too busy to consider getting one.

She and Jenny had been chattering nonstop for the past hour and Marissa was amazed at the instant connection she'd forged with the other woman as well as the dog. Normally, she did not make friends easily. Her competitive nature kept her on guard, wary of potential rivals. But Jenny possessed an open honesty that had Marissa loosening her tongue. She even found herself telling Jenny about getting dumped by Steve.

"I think he did you a favor by leaving. It sounds like you two didn't share the same values," Jenny said.

"What do you mean?" Marissa frowned.

Now, that was an odd thing to say. In her estimation she and Steve had been a great fit. They were both success-oriented workaholics. They liked nice things, were organized, efficient and competent. Everything had been just fine until Steve had gotten it into his head that she wasn't fun-loving enough to suit him.

"I don't know either of you, of course, but it seems to me like you need a man who values home and family and romance."

"Really? You drew that impression from me?"

Taken aback, Marissa could only stare. What on

earth made Jenny think that about her? She had always felt she needed a man who valued her power and independence and sense of order. Honestly, she didn't think she was very family oriented, and as a military brat she'd grown accustomed to rootlessness, although if pressed, she would confess to hungering for a romantic relationship that worked.

Jenny was about to reply, when the back door opened and Beau ambled in, a game of Twister tucked under his arm.

Immediately, her gaze was drawn to his casual, insouciant gait. Did the man have any idea how compellingly sexy he looked in the black, long-sleeved T-shirt hugging his broad shoulders, and those snug-fitting faded Levi's that enhanced even more fascinating parts of his anatomy?

Marissa shook her head, determined to empty her mind of such inappropriate thoughts. What on earth was the matter with her?

He pulled out a chair, turned it around and sat with the lattice-weave rattan back pressed against his chest. She caught a whiff of his scent—leather, sweet basil and gorgeous guy. She couldn't help noticing the silkiness of his dark brown windblown hair. She suppressed the disconcerting urge to reach out and tame the unruly strands with her fingers just to see if it was really as soft as it looked.

He tossed the Twister-game box onto the table.

What was this?

Marissa sent him a questioning expression. His sultry body heat upped the temperature in the room a good ten degrees and his proximity had her stomach doing erratic flips.

His grin was smug.

"I've given your proposition some thought," he said after a long pause.

"You're going to take the job?" She sat up straighter, her voice optimistic. Had she worn him down already?

"Not so fast." He raised his palm, holding it up like a stop sign.

Jenny had risen from the table to clear the dishes and she was standing directly behind Beau. She waved to catch Marissa's attention.

"Remember, don't rush him," Jenny mouthed silently.

Beau turned his head, but his sister quickly spun on her heel to deposit the dishes into the sink.

Right. Don't rush him.

During their cozy coffee klatch Jenny had reiterated that Beau moved at Beau's pace and nobody short of God could speed him up. Just thinking about allowing Beau to set the tempo of their interactions made her anxious. Marissa clenched her hands into fists and dropped them into her lap.

Play with him, Jenny had advised without having any idea just how hard it was for Marissa to engage in casual recreation.

Marissa had to bite down on her tongue to keep from breaking the silence. Even though the delay was excruciating she resisted the urge to grab him by the front of the shirt and demand he stop being coy. She forced a smile and waited for him to continue.

Just when she was beginning to believe the guy loved torturing her, he spoke.

"I admire your determination," Beau said. "I admit I was put out with you when you first showed up here. But then I figured if this business deal meant enough for you to hunt me down, I owed you the opportunity to let you try and convince me."

"Oh, thank you," Marissa said in a rush, the words tumbling from her lips. She leaned forward, her gaze intense, and clutched the edge of the table. "You won't regret this decision, Beau. I promise."

"Wait." He raised his palm again. Already she was beginning to hate that conversation-halting gesture. "You haven't heard me out."

She shifted in her seat. "I'm listening."

"Good."

Another annoying pause.

Get on with it already!

"You seem like the competitive sort, so I thought a challenge was in order."

"Oh?"

A challenge? Now, *this* she could get into.

He nodded. "If I win the challenge, you pack up and go back to New York."

"And if I win?"

"I'll take the job."

Marissa grinned. *Get ready to lose, sucker.* Dwight D. Sturgess had raised a serious competitor. Lucky for her, Beau didn't know that. Her promotion might as well be carved in stone.

"But," he cautioned, "only under one condition."

"What's the condition?" She frowned. This guy was complicated. He might act all languid and good-old-boyish, but the sharp, intelligent expression in his silver-gray eyes told her he possessed more layers than baklava.

"I'll tell you if you win."

"No, no, no." She shook her head. "I want to know where I stand right now."

He shrugged and started to get up. "Then the challenge is off."

"Wait, wait, wait." She reached out to place a restraining hand on his arm. "Okay. Have it your way. What does this challenge entail?"

He thumped the box on the table with his hand. "A game of Twister."

She made a face. "No fair. I've never played Twister before."

"Then it's high time you did."

"This is pretty lame, Thibbedeaux," she said, pushing the sleeves of her blouse up to her elbows. "Trying to chase me off with a sexy parlor game."

Bull's-eye.

She could tell by the gleam in his gaze that she had hit center target. He had been hoping she would decline to play, thereby putting the onus for quitting on her shoulders. Well, he hadn't counted on the persistence of Marissa Sturgess. She might be many things, but a quitter she was not.

"We could always play Spin the Bottle. Or maybe you'd prefer Post Office." He touched the tip of his tongue to his upper lip.

Marissa gritted her teeth and glared. "Twister is fine."

They stared at each. His silver-gray eyes hot, daring. The challenge had already begun.

"Jenny," Beau called to his sister over his shoulder. "Will you be the referee?"

Jenny cleared her throat. "You sure you want to do this, Marissa? Beau is a Twister master."

"Set up the game." Marissa's eyes never left Beau's face.

"My pleasure," Jenny said and picked up the Twister box.

They adjourned to the sitting room, generously decorated with Victorian-era antiques, and Jenny spread out the colorful plastic mat on the floor while Anna lay down to watch.

"What comes next?" Marissa asked.

"First things first," Beau said. "Let's get you out of those high-fashion torture devices you're wearing on your feet. No one can enjoy themselves in four-inch heels."

"Don't worry. I won't be enjoying myself with or without my shoes."

Beau just chuckled.

Jenny read the rules while they kicked off their shoes and squared off across from each other on opposite ends of the mat.

The rules turned out to be quite simple. Mainly it

seemed the key to winning was to possess good balance and flexibility. Thank heavens for her Wednesday-evening power-yoga class. She was going to happily kick Beau's booty and teach him a lesson he wouldn't soon forget.

Jenny perched on the arm of the sofa and flicked the spinner. "Right hand on red," she called out.

Beau and Marissa dived for the same red circle, their hands brushing as they went. At the contact, a tingle of electricity so strong it almost took her breath shot up her arm. Her initial instinct was to pull away, but she wasn't about to give up her circle. She bared her teeth at him and growled. Anna whined, startled by Marissa's fierceness.

"You're scaring the dog," Beau chided.

"So move."

"No way. You move."

"Marissa was there first, Beau," Jenny said. "You have to find another circle."

Marissa's feet were planted on the starting circles, her right hand slapped flat against the mat. Then that ratfink Beau angled for a red circle just beneath her breastbone, bringing his shoulder in contact with her upper arm. He had the audacity to look her squarely in the eye and wink.

She stuck out her tongue.

"Don't brandish that thing unless you intend on using it," he whispered.

"Get stuffed."

"Left leg on yellow," Jenny called out.

Marissa scissored her left leg around in search of

a yellow spot and in the process crashed into Beau's thigh. She teetered, right arm and right leg on the mat, left arm and left leg flailing in the air.

Please no, no. She couldn't lose her balance. Not this early in the game. How humiliating to be bested so quickly.

Dammit, why hadn't she insisted on changing out of this tight short-skirt before starting the game? If the man happened to turn his head in just the wrong direction he would be able to see clearly that she preferred thong undies.

She wobbled and her stationary knee threatened to buckle if she didn't get her other leg twisted around and on the ground soon.

Breathe. You're in control.

Her foot found the yellow circle and her body stabilized. She shot him a triumphant grin. Ha!

''Right leg blue,'' Jenny said.

Beau lunged for the same blue circle she moved toward.

''Get out of my territory,'' she snapped when he beat her to it, forcing her to lean over him to find another one. ''There are plenty of other spaces.''

''Throwing you off balance is all part of the plan. Strategy, strategy, strategy.''

Beau was obviously enjoying stoking her ire. The turkey.

Well, two could play that game.

In the meantime, her breasts were grazing his back and she could see he had a small half-moon scar on the side of his neck. She wondered how he'd gotten the scar and then hated herself for wondering. Plus, he smelled so damn good her mouth even started to water.

Stop it! Develop your line of attack. This is war. You're fighting for your dream job. You can't let this guy get the better of you.

Jenny thumped the spinner. The sound went off like a gunshot in Marissa's head.

When Jenny said, "Right leg green circle," she made sure she scooted to the green circle as far away from Beau as she could reach. The best defense might be a good offense but she had a feeling he was anticipating an aggressive move on her part, so she did the opposite of what he expected.

Instead, she retreated, luring him to her. Later, she would swoop in for the kill and he would never know what hit him, poor guy.

Not to mention, she was now thankfully out of range of his distractingly masculine body. Proximity to so much testosterone clouded a woman's decision-making process.

"Left arm blue circle."

Sheesh, she'd just gotten comfortable. Marissa moved even farther from Beau.

Right on cue, here he came after her, edging for the corner. He went low, angling toward the blue circle inches from her foot, foolishly putting himself in jeopardy by stretching extra wide in order to achieve his targeted goal.

Ah, men. Sometimes they were just too easy.

She had him right where she wanted him, unstable and ready to conquer.

''Left leg red.''

Marissa stretched out in front of Beau, making sure her blouse rose up enough to expose her bare midriff. Let him take a gander at that. She heard his raspy breathing, felt his warm air tickle her skin.

''Right arm blue circle.''

He inched toward her corner, Marissa slipped to the side. Her limbs were straining, exhausted by the contorted positions.

''Right leg red.''

Marissa swung around in front of him, claiming the closest red circle. Beau flailed, realizing at last he'd been set up.

''You wench,'' he said.

The only way he could reach a red circle was to reposition himself faceup. Slowly, he turned, careful not to remove his other limbs from their respective circles.

When he was done rearranging himself he was sprawled with his legs spread out, face pointed at the ceiling, his arms crisscrossed, his body wedged in the corner of the mat. It was a very awkward position to maintain.

His muscles quivered. Sweat beaded his forehead.

Marissa grinned. Victory!

You're mine now, Beau. All mine.

When Jenny called out, ''Right arm green circle,'' Marissa went in to close the deal.

Jaw set, muscles tensed, she moved quickly, leaning over him to claim the green circle to the left of his head, effectively pinning him in. There was no way he could reach another green circle without losing his balance. Not with her in his way, hovering above him.

"Run out of moves, Thibbedeaux?"

She met his gaze and narrowed her eyes in triumph. His chest rose and fell in a jerky rhythm. Marissa realized she too was breathing hard.

And then, he chuckled.

"What's so funny?" she demanded.

"You."

"What's funny about me?"

"Nothing." He gave her a lopsided grin and shook his head.

"You're enjoying making a fool of me. That's why you forced me to play this stupid game."

"I didn't force you. You chose to participate of your own free will."

"You think I'm a big joke."

"I don't."

"So stop laughing."

"I can't."

"Why not?"

"For one thing, I'm having a good time. News flash, it's what people do when they're enjoying themselves. For another, you're so friggin' intense. I've never seen anyone play Twister with such vengeance. Relax, Marissa, it's just a game."

"A game I intend on winning," she said, irritated with him for poking fun at her.

So she was intense. So what? What was it with men wanting her to relax? Why did every guy under the sun, save for her father, seem to think intensity was such a grave sin?

"You really think so?"

"I know so. Now move your right arm to a green circle."

"Nope."

"You can't just wobble here."

"I can."

His lips were millimeters away. Full, firm lips that irrationally snagged her attention.

"You're going down. You might as well surrender," she said.

His muscles were really trembling now. It wouldn't take much. She lusted for that promotion and one way or the other he was going to make it happen for her. She needed a way to send him sprawling.

What would take him by surprise? What would he least expect? What was her best weapon? What would render him helpless?

Her mind was so occupied with just how to tip him over the edge, that she lost her concentration. When the dastard man turned the tables and blew into her ear, her left knee buckled, but she managed to catch herself just before she hit the floor.

"Cheater."

"Hey, all's fair in love and Twister."

That did it. He was challenging her to call out the big guns. If he wanted to play dirty, he'd picked the wrong gal.

"Oh buddy, you are so screwed."

"How so?" He wriggled an eyebrow.

"How this."

And then she lowered her head, dropped her lips to his and kissed him.

5

HOLY MOTHER of Bourbon Street.

Beau's plan to chase Marissa back to New York melted away like cold butter on a hot biscuit.

In unison, his arms and legs collapsed. He fell flat on his back, and Marissa, done in by his downward momentum, tumbled on top of him.

His arms went around her waist and he pulled her tight against his chest.

Gotcha.

Her small eyes rounded wide and she started to draw back, but he wasn't about to let her go. He wanted more of those lips.

Slowly, leisurely, he increased the pressure, deepening the kiss, coaxing her lips apart with his inquisitive tongue.

He didn't remember that his little sister and his dog were watching them. He didn't recall that he'd just lost the bet and he might have to create a sex video game. Hell, he nearly forgot his own name.

Only one thought throbbed through his brain.

Marissa, Marissa, Marissa.

With a long, lazy flick of his tongue, he seduced her in deliberate degrees. His head spun with the dizzying flavor of her. As he'd expected, she tasted exquisitely rich and satisfying.

He took the kiss deeper. He groaned low in his throat and she responded with a helpless mewling. The soft sound was an instant trigger, powering up his testosterone. What stunned Beau most of all was that Marissa was going along with him, escalating their kiss. He felt her body relax against his chest.

Apparently, he hadn't been wrong about their mutual sexual attraction.

His palm caressed the curve of her hip and an instant masculine response surged through his body. Her skirt was so short he could feel the hem of it hiked up against the back of her thigh. Her mouth was moist and hot and the spot where his hand rested grew warmer. He heard the tempo of her breathing accelerate.

"Ahem." Jenny cleared her throat. "I'll just shut the parlor door on my way out."

Regretfully, he broke the kiss but the imprint of Marissa's lips, the heady taste of her, lingered like evening dew at sunrise.

The sound of the door shutting softly and Anna's dog tags jingling told them their audience had left the room.

Marissa scrambled to her feet and then extended her hand to help him up. When Beau was standing, their gazes locked, their hands still interlaced, she touched the tip of her wicked tongue to her upper lip.

"I win," she whispered. "You've got to design the video game for Pegasus."

Losing wasn't so bad, he thought with an inward grin. Not when the benefits far outweighed the punishment.

"Have you forgotten?" he asked, surprised to hear his own voice sounding so raspy. "I said if you won I would design the game only under one condition. This isn't a done deal, Marissa. You might find my stipulation unacceptable."

"You're counting on me finding it unacceptable, aren't you? Come on, Thibbedeaux. Lay it on me. What's it going to take to get you to say yes to this project?"

"You know I'm not leaving Louisiana, not for a week, not for a day, not for an hour."

"Is that your condition?" She waved away his refusal to leave home as inconsequential. "That's no problem. We can work through e-mail and teleconferencing. I can even make a few trips back and forth if necessary."

He shook his head. "Nope, sorry. That's not good enough."

"Why not?"

"I need more from you."

"Stop being cryptic. I find it annoying."

"Oh, you do?"

Beau liked riling her up. Not that it was such a tall order. She stayed ready for a fight. He saw it in the aggressive tilt of her shoulders, in the defensive way she jumped to conclusions. Six weeks with him and he could remedy her pugilistic tendencies.

He thought of how much his life had changed for

the better since he left New York, and he longed to give her the same gift of tranquillity he'd discovered for himself. And in the process he hoped they'd both have a hell of a good time. Would she agree to his proposition?

"Beau, please," she wheedled, trying a different tactic. She batted her eyelashes but he wasn't fooled. The woman was a competitor all the way. "Don't tease. What is it you want?"

"You."

"Me?" Her voice went up an octave and she splayed a palm across her chest.

"Hands on all the way. This is our project. Together. You and me. I won't do it without you."

"What are you saying? You want me to help you design the game?"

"That and so much more."

"How much more?" She raised a wary eyebrow.

"I want you here in Louisiana with me. Twenty-four/seven for the duration of the entire project, about six weeks."

"And that's it?"

"What do you think?" He half lowered his eyelids and gave her his most seductive look.

"Are you suggesting what I'm thinking you're suggesting?"

"What are you thinking?"

They were going around in circles, neither one of them wanting to come right out and say it. They had eyes only for each other and they were both breathing so rapidly a doctor would have prescribed an inhaler.

But asthma medicine wouldn't cure what was ailing them both.

"I'm wondering why you want me."

"For starters," he said, his gaze pinned to those sumptuous brown eyes. "You are in more dire need of fun than anyone I've ever met. If the goal of this video game is to help uptight people relax, then you'll be the perfect test case. If it works on you, it'll work on anyone."

"You're saying we'll be creating this game together. Exploring. Experimenting. Learning as we go?" she said, still circling the topic, carefully choosing her words.

"That's what I'm saying."

"You know my involvement here could never be anything more than temporary. You totally understand that, don't you?"

"Understand it and accept it." He telegraphed his desire for her through his eyes, sending her the message that he found her completely and utterly irresistible.

"Nobody gets hurt."

"Right." He nodded, his heart thumping, his chest tightening.

"Just fun and games."

"That's what this assignment is about."

"Good. Just so we have that straight. I have to phone my boss and make sure he's on board with me being gone for so long."

"Okay."

An awkward silence stretched between them. Marissa curled a finger over her shoulder. "I'm just going to go make the call."

"You do that," he said.

She turned, picked up her high heels and headed for the door, her fanny swishing provocatively. That's when Beau realized he'd just covertly committed to having his first no-strings-attached fling.

JUST WHAT in the hell *was* Beau Thibbedeaux proposing?

His answer rumbled through in her head. "You are in more dire need of fun than anyone I've ever met. If the goal of this video game is to help uptight people relax, then you'll be the perfect test case. If it works on you, it'll work on anyone."

Meaning what exactly? He was going to try out his foreplay moves on her and then if they were successful, incorporate them into the video game?

She hadn't asked him the question directly, even though it had hung heavily in the air between them, because she didn't want to hear the answer.

She knew it was yes.

Marissa paced the length of the Scarlett O'Hara Room, arms folded across her chest, the Pegasus contract rolled up in her right fist. Should she do this? Was it smart? Was she in effect using her body to get what she wanted? It wasn't a pretty thought.

But she was attracted to Beau. More attracted than she had been to any man in a very long time. Was it so wrong to enjoy herself on the job? They were both adults. It's not as if they'd ever see each other again once the assignment was finished.

And then there was the issue Steve had brought up. This might be the perfect occasion to prove to herself that sex wasn't a serious deal for her, that she could indeed have fun in bed.

So this is about getting even with Steve?

No. It was about making sure they created the best product for Baxter and Jackson. It was about experimentation and trying something different. It was about getting in touch with her whimsical side.

If she had one.

Frustration burned a hole in her stomach because she was waffling. She wasn't a waffler. She didn't even like waffles.

So why hadn't she immediately accepted Beau's condition and whipped out the contract on the spot? Signing him was what she wanted. Why had she used Judd as an excuse? Why did she have the sudden urge to sprint to her rental car and drive away as fast as she could?

Because you're afraid.

Afraid? Ha. She wasn't afraid. What did she have to be afraid of?

Oh let's see, whispered the annoying little voice in the back of her head. *That you'll want to kiss those delicious lips of his again.*

Absentmindedly, she reached up and fingered her mouth still tingling from their kiss. She wasn't afraid of kissing him. She liked kissing him.

Maybe you're afraid of where all that kissing might lead.

Actually, she wasn't afraid of that, either. A shiver of delight scampered up her spine at the image of Beau in her bed. She thought about his lopsided easygoing smile, his slow-motion swagger, his long lean legs and sinful silver-gray eyes.

Nope, she wasn't afraid of physical intimacy, although a wild sexual fling with a contract employee was probably not the smartest idea in the world.

Okeydokey, how's this? Maybe you're worried that if you stay down here the slow pace will rub off on you and you'll lose your competitive edge.

Marissa gnawed the inside of her cheek. Nah, she couldn't lose her competitive edge in just a few weeks. Could she?

Maybe the honest reason is you're terrified Beau will see right through you and discover you're not as successful and put together as you pretend to be.

Shut up!

With a sharp toss of her head, she banished the nasty voice to the darkest corner of her brain.

Stay or go? She tapped the rolled-up contract against her forehead.

Waffle, waffle, waffle.

She knew how to end this quandary. She plunked down on the bed, reached for the phone on the bedside table and called Judd.

"Marissa, how goes it?" Judd's hearty voice boomed in her ear. "You sign Thibbedeaux yet?"

"Um. I'm afraid it's a little more complicated than I foresaw."

That was the understatement of the century. Marissa rubbed the nape of her neck and tried to blot out the knowledge that Beau seemed to know exactly what she needed. His perceptiveness scared the panties off her.

"He rejected you," Judd said flatly and then swore under his breath. "Well, I'm sure you gave it your best shot."

"He didn't reject me. Not exactly." Restlessly, she dog-eared the top page of the contract, but then straightened it again.

"Oh?" Judd perked up. "What exactly?"

"He has certain conditions."

"What kind of conditions?"

Marissa told him.

Judd said nothing.

"Well?" she ventured at last.

"Why would he want you to stay in Louisiana?" Judd asked.

Marissa shrugged even though he couldn't see her. "He thinks I need to learn how to relax."

"Let me guess. He's applied for the job of your relaxation coach."

"Something like that."

"Hmm."

"Hmm, what?"

"Marissa, I can't tell you how far to go in order to close this deal, but you know how much the Baxter and Jackson account means to Pegasus."

"Yes, yes."

"And may I remind you that you did make Francine Phillips and I a solemn oath."

"I know. I know. But if I stay here it means I'll be out of the office for six weeks or more." *It also means I'll probably do something really stupid, like taking Beau Thibbedeaux to bed and losing my bet with Dash.* In that moment, she prayed Judd would let her off the hook and tell her to come home. "I don't want to inconvenience you guys," she said.

"We'll miss you, of course, but we'll manage."

"You want me to do this."

She swallowed hard. She felt the noose closing tighter. She'd hung herself by making promises she was afraid to keep. Maybe she could talk to Beau again, get him to rescind his ridiculous request.

"The ultimate decision is yours," Judd said. "But I must tell you, Dash has been busy since you left. He's already brought in two new clients."

"In two days!"

"He's gunning for you, and if you decide not to pursue Thibbedeaux, then I'm afraid I'll have to give the account directorship to him."

GIRDING HER COURAGE, Marissa picked up the frayed contract and went to find Beau. She didn't know why her pulse should be pounding so hard, but it was.

She found Jenny in the lobby checking in a middle-aged German couple who were busy oohing and aahing over the rocking chairs.

Jenny waved her over to the counter. "So, did Beau agree to design the video game for you?"

Marissa held up the contract. "Do you know where he went? I knocked on his bedroom door but got no answer."

"He's down at the Lingo Lounge."

"The Lingo Lounge?"

"It's a bar just this side of Main Street."

"He's in a bar at..." Marissa consulted her watch. "Two o'clock in the afternoon?"

"He's playing in a pool tournament."

"Oh, that makes it so much better."

Jenny struggled to suppress a smile and shook her head.

"What's so funny?" Marissa asked.

"Beau's going to have his hands full with you."

"Or I'm going to have my hands full of him," Marissa said, and then realizing her Freudian slip, quickly amended, "I mean with him, with him."

Jenny just giggled and turned to help the German couple with their luggage.

To Marissa's surprise the Lingo Lounge turned out to be rather trendy with designer beer on tap and an extensive wine list. The front room had chairs and sofas grouped in conversational arrangements around a gas fireplace.

The second room featured the bar and dance floor and beyond that lay the pool hall. From the Wurlitzer, Faith Hill sang about the transcendent experience of a wondrous kiss. Involuntarily, Marissa's fingers went to caress her lips.

As she walked through the bar, she noticed that the men draped from the bar stools were ogling her, but she put on her best bored-New Yorker face and stalked right past them without so much as a glance in their direction.

She stopped short, however, when she entered the poolroom. It was her turn to ogle.

There, in all its blue-jeaned glory, was Beau's rump sticking up in the air.

Oh my.

Beau was bent over the closest pool table, pool cue in hand.

Estrogen, that troublemaking bitch, chomped into her with unabashed glee. Estrogen didn't care if Mr. Testosterone bundle over there had the potential to wreak havoc with her life. Estrogen wanted what she wanted when she wanted it and the consequences be damned.

The three other guys clustered around Beau suddenly stood up straighter and sucked in their guts. One guy ran his hand through his hair. Another adjusted his belt. The third, a whip-thin man with a lean-and-hungry look, started inching around the table toward her.

"Hello there, *chère*," he drawled in a heavy Cajun accent. "What brings you into my fantasies?"

"Back off, Ace," Beau said, never turning his head in Marissa's direction. "She's with me."

All three men looked crestfallen.

"Damn, Beau," Ace grumbled. "You get all the good ones."

Beau made his shot, and then straightened to meet Marissa's eyes.

"How did you know it was me?" she asked, stunned by the heady impact of their gazes colliding.

"Because when these three goons started drooling in unison, I figured it had to be the prettiest woman in town standing behind me." Beau's lopsided grin took her breath away.

Don't you dare blush, Marissa Jane.

"He's feedin' you a line of bull, *chère*." Ace tipped his cap. "We spotted you out on the street before you came in."

"Are you always in a bar?" she asked Beau, determined to turn the tables and make him uncomfortable.

"I wasn't in a bar this morning," he pointed out.

"That's because they don't have a bed in one," she replied tartly. "Or I imagine you would have been."

Ace chortled. "Actually, Harmon keeps a cot in the storeroom for his favorite customers who've had too much to drink. What say you and I borrow it?" The thin man gave her such an exaggerated leer, Marissa almost laughed in his face.

"Ace," Beau growled. "I suggest you back off. Now."

"Could I speak with you in private, please?" she asked Beau pointedly.

"But of course."

The three guys let loose with catcalls.

"Shut up," Beau said pleasantly.

"You leaving, you forfeitin'." Ace angled a head at the pool table.

"Don't you think she's worth it?" Beau asked his buddies.

The three nodded solemnly.

Marissa rolled her eyes as Beau took her by the elbow and guided her out the side exit.

Nonchalantly, he leaned against the brick building and raked his gaze over her body. She felt jaybird naked. Did the guy have X-ray vision or what?

"Well?" he asked.

"I spoke with my boss," she said.

"And?"

"He's authorized me to stay in Louisiana until the project is completed."

"Throwing you to the wolf, is he? I figured as much." Beau nodded.

"What are you talking about?"

"Sealing the deal with me is more important to your boss than your virtue."

"No, it's not," Marissa denied, even though the hard knot in the pit of her stomach acknowledged he spoke the truth. "And it's my virtue to do with what I will. My boss isn't making me do anything. I want to stay here."

What had she expected of Judd? To tell her to get her fanny back home to New York? That no way would he allow her to work with a man who slipped sexual provisos into his contract? She was a grown woman, she knew how the world worked.

"Sure you do. Spending weeks in Fleur de Luna, Louisiana, is your deepest dream come true."

She wanted to say spending weeks in his bed was her deepest dream come true, but she didn't. It was strictly estrogen talking and she knew it. "Don't mock me."

"I'm not mocking you. I'm mocking me."

She cocked her head and studied him a long moment. His eyes looked strangely sad. "Let's be honest. Why do you really want me to stay?"

"You want me to spell it out."

She gulped. "Yes."

"Because I need you."

"Need me?" she squeaked.

"Not necessarily in a sexual way." His easy grin was back, the sad expression vanished from his eyes. "Although, I wouldn't be opposed to exploring what happened back there in the parlor. You're one hell of a kisser."

"You're not so bad yourself."

"If you could just relax a little, you could be world-class."

Marissa made an impatient noise low in her throat. "Will you knock off with the relaxing stuff? Maybe I don't want to be a world-class kisser."

"Princess, I can tell by the look in your eyes you've got a hunger to be a world-class everything."

"Don't call me Princess, and for the record, I like being tense and uptight and stressed out. It suits me, okay?"

He raised his palms. "Okay."

"So, in what way do you 'need' me?"

"Frankly, I don't know if I can create a game on my own anymore. Not in a timely manner. Not without someone cracking the whip."

"You're asking me to stand over you and crack the whip?"

He closed his eyes briefly and swallowed so hard his Adam's apple bobbed. "Yeah."

"What is it? Why do you have that strange look on your face."

"I just got an incredible visual. You. A whip. Thigh-high black boots and a red garter belt."

"This is sexual harassment, you know."

"Only if you don't like it. Do you like it?"

"No," she lied.

He shrugged. "Sorry. I can't help what flashes through my mind."

"You can help telling me about it."

"Hey, you asked."

Marissa shoved both hands through her hair and then slowly blew out her breath. She fought to control her own mental fantasies, struggled not to say to hell with it and just kiss him again.

"If we're going to be working together, we need to face this attraction head-on," she said.

"I couldn't agree with you more."

"We've got a certain chemistry going on here, I'm not denying it."

"Me, either."

"But we both know a physical relationship between us would be counterproductive. Right?"

"I'm not following that line of reasoning."

"We've got work to do."

"Work that entails creating a sex game. What would be more natural than taking things a step further?"

"Yes, but it's work nonetheless." She fidgeted, shifting her weight from foot to foot.

"We're going to be exploring some deep sexual fantasies together. Are you trying to tell me you want to keep our libidos on a leash?"

"I'm glad you understand."

"Well then, if you can keep your hands to yourself, so can I."

"I'm happy to hear it."

"And if we happen to cross the line over the course of the next few weeks, then it'll be because you initiated it," he said.

"I won't initiate anything."

"We'll see."

"I won't," she insisted, but even as she denied it, estrogen was just itching to unbutton his shirt and splay her horny fingers over his manly chest.

The intensity of the cravings shocked her and made Marissa want to jump into her rented T-bird and drive all the way back to Manhattan without stopping once. She hated this scary, out-of-control feeling. She'd never experienced anything quite like it.

"Okay," he said. "I believe you won't initiate anything."

She cleared her throat and pulled the contract from her purse. She was a professional, dammit. She could and would resist this man. No matter how charming. No matter how much her body ached to sleep with him.

"Now that we have all the formalities out of the way, I just need for you to sign on the dotted line."

"Your wish, Princess," he said, inflection on the word *princess*, "is my command."

6

_____

"SO, WHAT'S GOING ON with Miss Manhattan?"
Remy asked Beau several hours later. "Jenny called
and told me she showed up at the B and B and you
were acting all googly-eyed and weird."

"Miss Manhattan?" Remy's petite, dark-haired
wife, Allie, looked up from placing her world-class
jambalaya on the dinner table.

"If you ask me," Remy teased, "she's out of your
league."

"What's my husband jawin' about?" Allie wiped
her fingers on her apron and took her seat beside her
husband. "Have you got a new girlfriend, Beau?"

After leaving the Lingo Lounge, Beau had been too
keyed up to go back to Greenbrier and risk running
into Marissa before he'd had time to think this whole
thing through, so he'd taken the twenty-minute drive
over to Remy's house.

"Uncle Beau's gotta girlfriend?" his seven-year-
old niece, Sarah, asked. "What's her name?"

"Yeah." Allie grinned. "What's her name?"

"Her name is Marissa and she's not my girlfriend," Beau denied. He was starting to feel ganged

up on. Sometimes families could be a royal pain in the butt, no matter how much you loved them.

"Marissa and Beau, sitting in a tree, k-i-s-s-i-n-g," Sarah chanted.

"Girls." Six-year-old Willis scowled as his dad spooned jambalaya onto his plate. "Yuck."

Beau clamped his nephew on the shoulder and thought of the way Marissa ran simultaneous hot and cold. "You got a point, buddy. Sometime girls can be pretty yucky."

"Hey!" Allie and Sarah protested in unison.

"Why dontcha invent a video game where all the girls are extinct, Uncle Beau," Willis suggested. "Like the dinosaurs."

"One of these days, son." Remy winked at his wife. "Girls aren't going to seem so yucky to you."

"Well, Mom's not yucky. You could keep moms in the video game, but sisters have got to go."

"No, Uncle Beau." Sarah glared at Willis. "Do one without stupid baby brothers."

"I'm afraid I won't have much time to design brotherless and sisterless videos games for a while," Beau said, piling jambalaya onto his own plate with gusto.

"You dog." Remy grinned and passed a basket of jalapeño hush puppies around the table. "You accepted Miss Manhattan's job. Good for you."

"Hey, you were tired of me hanging out at the bar, I thought I'd give you a break," Beau said. "Besides, she made me an offer I couldn't refuse."

"I'll bet." Remy's grin widened and he wriggled

his eyebrows suggestively. "I saw the way you two sizzled. Whew-ee."

Beau couldn't help grinning back. "*Sizzle* isn't the word for it."

"Fellas," Allie said and cocked her head in the direction of the children. "Little pitchers and all that, but later, I'll want serious details."

"Yes, ma'am." Beau laughed, and as everyone gave their complete attention to the delicious food, he realized that for the first time in months he was truly excited about something.

Later, when the kids were in bed and he and Remy and Allie sat in the family room sipping sweet Moscato d'Asti with the European after-dinner tradition of cheese and fruit, Beau told all.

Normally, he wasn't the sort of guy who made his romantic intentions public fodder, but he couldn't seem to help himself. He wanted to talk about Marissa and he wanted to get Allie's perspective on the situation.

"I've never met anyone wired so tight," Beau told Allie. "She reminds me of the way I used to be before I crashed and burned."

"Did you take the job for her or for yourself?" Allie asked.

"Both, I suppose. She's very persuasive and you guys were right. I have been pretty directionless since we finished renovating Greenbrier. Plus, I get this feeling that deep down inside, Marissa isn't all that happy with her life, even though she can't see it."

"Uh-oh." Allie tucked her bare feet underneath her and shook her head.

"Uh-oh what?"

"Sounds like you've got a little savior syndrome going on there."

"What do you mean?"

"You see in Marissa all the things that were wrong in your life and you want to show her the way. Have you considered the possibility that she likes the path she's on, that she might not appreciate your interfering?"

"It occurred to me."

"But you're going to do it anyway." Remy put his arm around Allie's shoulder and drew her closer to him.

"If she could just slow down a little. Relax. Have fun. Surrender to the moment."

"Sounds to me like a four-point plan for seduction," Remy said.

"That's how you caught me." Allie burrowed against Remy's chest. "I was a sucker for that slow languid drawl of yours and those moonlight canoe rides."

"Yep, Surrender was your middle name."

They grinned at each other and Remy fed Allie a piece of cheese. They'd been high-school sweethearts and married right after graduation and nine years later they still acted like newlyweds. Beau envied what they'd found with each other and he wondered sadly if he would ever have that kind of emotional closeness.

"So," Allie said. "Let me get all this straight. She's all business, you're all fun. She loves Manhattan and you're rooted in Louisiana. She's fast-paced and you make a snail look lively. You two are going to be designing a sex video game together for the next six weeks or longer. You've got this powerful sexual chemistry going on. Hmm, I'd say you have the perfect recipe for a red-hot, opposites-collide fling."

"My thoughts exactly," Remy concurred. "Go for it, dude."

"I do foresee one problem, however." Allie wagged a finger.

"What's that?"

"You're not a red-hot-fling sort of guy."

"I'm thinking maybe it's time I tried something new," Beau said.

"You know, Allie's right. You do have a tendency to think sex means love," Remy said. "They're not always one and the same."

"That's exactly my point. I want to learn to separate the two. This thing with Marissa seems to afford us both the opportunity to mutually satisfy our needs. If things indeed even go that far."

"If it were anybody else..." Allie shrugged. "I'd say dive in and have a good time. But we love you, Beau and we'd hate to see you get hurt."

"I won't get hurt. I'm a grown man. I'm going into this situation with my eyes open. Besides, who knows? It could end up being just a harmless flirtation. I did promise Marissa nothing would happen unless she initiated it."

"Oh," Allie said. "I get it. Her mouth is saying no, no, no, but her body is saying yes, yes, yes."

"Something like that. She's worried that a sexual relationship might compromise our work relationship."

"Well," his brother said, "if it does turn out to be more than a harmless flirtation and that big tough New York dame breaks your heart, we're here for you, bro." Remy patted his own shoulder. "You can always come crying to us."

THE FOLLOWING MORNING, at 7:00 a.m. sharp, Marissa knocked on Beau's bedroom door. She was dressed for a day at the office, blue pin-striped power suit, high-necked silver blouse and her new Jimmy Choos.

Her makeup was purposefully understated and she clutched her laptop and briefcase under her arm. She'd already eaten a breakfast of bagels and fresh fruit with Jenny and some of the other B and B guests and she was ready to get down to work.

When Beau didn't answer, she knocked more forcefully. She didn't know how long he had lingered at the Lingo Lounge after she'd departed the previous afternoon with a signed copy of the amended contract clutched triumphantly in her hand, but surely the man wasn't hungover on a Thursday morning.

She waited a moment. When she got no further response, Marissa tried twisting the knob, but the door was locked. "Thibbedeaux, get up. This is me, cracking the whip."

She heard the sound of bare feet padding across the hardwood floor. The door opened a crack and she caught sight of a rumpled Beau, his hair sticking straight up, one bleary but very cute gray eye and a mint-green sheet wrapped around his tanned, lean waist.

It was January, for crying out loud. Where on earth had the man obtained such a beach-burnished glow in the dead of winter? He didn't look like the tanning-bed type. She figured it must just be his natural coloring.

"Move aside," she said, marshaling her determination.

"Why didn't you tell me you were that desperate to get into my bed?" he drawled.

She was going to ignore his sexual innuendo. In the wee hours of the night, when she'd found herself staring at the ceiling, not sleeping and thinking too much of Beau, she'd made the decision. No matter how much he teased and smiled and cajoled, she would remain strictly professional. Absolutely no hanky-panky.

"Let's get down to work," she said briskly and made a point not to stare at his broad chest.

"I've got to warn you—" his voice rumbled low and suggestive in his chest "—I'm totally naked beneath this sheet."

"Sounds like a personal problem to me," Marissa quipped, even though her pulse was pumping like a boomtown oil well.

She deposited her briefcase and laptop on the antique writing desk where his computer sat and leaned over to look for a place to plug in.

I won't let him rattle me. If I stay cool, he'll eventually realize he's not going to get to me and he'll stop testing my limits.

"What," he asked, "are you wearing?"

"Much more than you." Straightening, she turned to face him.

The minute she got a second look at his naked chest, she experienced a deep abiding urge to run into the bathroom and splash cold water in her face. But Marissa wasn't about to let him know exactly how much he affected her.

"I'm sorry," Beau said, his eyes sparkling with pure mischief. "But I simply can't work under these conditions."

"What are you babbling on about?" She frowned.

"You. Dressed like that." He waved his free hand at her outfit.

"What's wrong with what I'm wearing?" she asked at the same time her eyes trailed helplessly over his buff body again.

Six-pack, hell. An entire case rippled his man's flat, sexy abdomen. Michelangelo's *David* dreamed of being so sculpted.

"Your clothes cover too much. You're buttoned up tighter than a Puritan spinster at a nudist colony."

"This is a business meeting. I'm dressed for business. You, however, are more appropriately attired for the nudist colony."

He laughed and shook his head. "I don't 'do' business. I don't work. I play. Besides, lest you forget, we're designing a sex video game.''

Like she could forget that fact for one single second. "That might be the case, but this is still—"

"Go change," he interrupted.

"Excuse me?"

"Go change."

"Who died and made you king?" His bossiness thrilled her and the scuttling thrill freaked her out.

She should not like this. Not at all. Why *did* she like this? What was wrong with her?

"I think Baxter and Jackson did. They wanted me as the designer and as the designer I want you to do what I say. Got a problem with that?"

Marissa gulped. A sharp, unexpected hunger stirred inside her. Face it, the man was a sex fantasy sprung to life with that just-tumbled-out-of-bed thing going on for him.

Dammit. She had to stop ogling him.

But his relaxed stance and his somnolent expression made her acutely aware of the unmade bed stretching out to her right. She couldn't let him get away with this. She would not give him the upper hand. Parcel out an inch and the infuriating man would undoubtedly take a mile. She hardened her jaw and narrowed her eyes.

"How about if I take off my jacket and undo the top button of my blouse. Would that satisfy?"

"Nope. Not good enough."

"Why not?"

"You ask too many questions."

"And you have too many demands," she said.

"Hey, if you want me to tear up that contract..."
He shrugged.

Blackmailer.

She glowered at him. "No, no. I'll go change."

"Wear something casual, something flirty, something feminine."

"I don't have anything like that. Business attire is all I brought with me."

"No casual clothes, no workie."

"Why don't I just go get a sheet of my own," she retorted. "Would that be casual enough for you, oh Lord of the Video Games?"

"Now you're just toying with me."

"Isn't that your thing? You like to play around."

"Princess, you have no idea. But if you keep tempting me, you're going to find out the hard way." He put impish emphasis on the word *hard*.

Startled, Marissa realized he was right. She was tempting him, trying to see how far he would push this game. He had answered her rather subconscious challenge with a decidedly calculated dare of his own.

She shook her head. What was happening to her? It must be all this clear fresh air clogging her brain.

She'd awoken that morning with a staunch resolution. She was going to do whatever it took to drive this project through in the shortest amount of time possible. She'd dressed with the express purpose of keeping things strictly professional and now here Beau was, trying his best to derail her plans, and damn if she wasn't actively participating in her own downfall.

He was watching her, waiting to see what she would do. His eyes gleamed in anticipation and she suddenly realized the outrageous man was picturing her naked.

"Stop it!"

"Stop what?"

"Imagining what I look like in a sheet."

"Oh, sweetheart, in my mind's eye, believe me, there is no sheet."

Twin spheres of heat rose to her cheeks and she ducked her head.

Calm. She had to remain calm. She could not, under any circumstances, let this man know exactly how much he rattled her. The main thing here was to get the project up on its legs. If blue jeans and a flouncy blouse were what it took to light a fire under him, then that's what she would wear.

"About those clothes," he said, reading her mind with infuriating accuracy. "You'll have to borrow some things from Jenny. Later on, we can go shopping in New Orleans."

"All right," she said. "I'll do it."

Momentarily, he looked taken aback by her easy acquiescence. Had he been braced for a fight? Was he disappointed or relieved that she'd caved so quickly?

She moved toward the hallway and that's when Marissa realized Beau was standing in front of the door, blocking her from making a clean getaway. In order to escape the room, she would have to squeeze past him.

"In the name of speeding things up," she said, clearing her throat and purposely not meeting his eyes, "I'll bring your breakfast up to you. Now, get in the shower. I'll be right back."

When in doubt, go on the offensive. The General had drilled that lesson into her head.

She edged toward the door.

"When I said I needed you to crack the whip over me, I didn't mean literally," Beau said.

"No?"

"The creative process can't be hurried or forced. It has to be coaxed, cajoled, invited to come play."

"Okay, okay, Mr. Lazybones. Have it your way." Marissa reached for the doorknob. "I get it, I get it."

His hand snaked out and grabbed her wrist, the heat of his fingers searing her every tendon, every ligament, every nerve fiber. "I don't think you do."

Inhaling sharply, she forced herself to meet his gaze when peering into those fascinating silver-gray orbs was the last thing on earth she wanted to do. She couldn't allow him to intimidate her. She was in charge and she wasn't about to let him forget it, no matter how creative and talented the guy might be.

But when she looked into his eyes something weird happened. All her bravado, all her forward momentum, all her strength of will just vanished, and in that one brief moment, she was left stripped of all her defenses.

And her pretenses.

In that moment, he was just a man and she was just a woman.

Beau's eyes were mercurial, changing from a glistening smoky gray to a dark smoldering silver, the color a tantalizing compliment to his ebony lashes and rich, dark eyebrows.

His full lips quirked up at the corners as he shot her what she was quickly starting to recognize as his trademark slow-down-darlin' grin. He might appear laid-back and easygoing, but beneath that languid exterior, she detected a current of something hot and taut and incredibly alive. The man was raw dynamite.

The heat of her own breath warmed her chin and she realized her lips were parted and she was breathing through her mouth as she stared endlessly into his eyes. She was hooked, hung on the barb of his intense, intelligent gaze, and heaven help her, she couldn't look away.

She was seriously screwed. Marissa realized with a sinking sensation. She wanted him to kiss her.

In fact, she had longed for a repeat performance since she'd kissed him yesterday morning in the parlor in order to win the Twister game. All night long, she had dreamed of his kisses, dreamed of tasting him again, dreamed of losing herself in his embrace.

And now, here he was, standing beside her, his hand on her wrist, his gaze glued to hers, wearing nothing but a bedsheet and the sexiest damn smile she had ever laid eyes on.

How easy it would be to drag him over to the bed,

straddle his massive erection, vividly visible beneath the thin sheet, and make love to him.

How easy and yet how utterly complicated.

She shouldn't. She couldn't. She wouldn't.

Kiss me, she thought. Kiss me, kiss me, kiss me.

Beau moistened his mouth.

Marissa flicked out the tip of her tongue to wet her own lips.

He lowered his head.

Her heart jumped out of her chest and into her throat.

His face was so close she could almost feel the brush of his beard stubble against her cheek.

Kiss me, kiss me, kiss me.

He pressed his mouth to her ear.

She closed her eyes and leaned into him. Her body tense…waiting, wanting, willing.

''I told you that you've got to be the one to initiate this. The ball, so to speak, is in your court,'' he said and then let her go.

7

BEAU STOOD in the shower, gritting his teeth as ice-cold water sluiced over his head and rolled down his back, but the chilly temperature did nothing to ease the desert heat radiating throughout his body.

Nor did it reduce the burgeoning size of his rock-hard erection. He could only pray he'd flustered her as much as she'd flustered him.

The magnetic pull, the longing from deep inside him, reined Beau up short. His body shuddered hard at the memory of his showdown with Marissa.

He rested his forehead against the wall of the shower stall as he recalled the peachy feel of her soft skin beneath his rough fingers, the gut-churning womanly scent of her in his nostrils, the sight of those cute little chocolate-brown eyes narrowing to mere slits in defiant challenge.

He was in over his head with this one, but what a way to drown.

His cock ached and throbbed. He gulped. This was his own fault.

When Marissa had leaned into him for the briefest of moments, he had known at once she was subconsciously giving him permission to haul her over to the bed, even if she didn't come right out and say she wanted him. He had practically drooled all over himself at the glorious prospect.

It had taken every ounce of control he possessed, but he had resisted temptation. The timing wasn't right. If he consummated things too soon, nothing would change for her. If he hoped to achieve his goal of helping her to slow down and learn to stop and sniff the daffodils, then he had to get her to relax. Not only relax, but to let down her guard and really see how she'd been deceiving herself. How she'd been equating success with self-worth. If he took her too soon, nothing would be different.

For either of them.

At that moment, Beau realized something startling. He might have convinced himself he was Marissa's salvation when in actuality the opposite was true. She was the one with the power to bring meaning back into his work. For the first time in two years, Beau acknowledged how much he wanted the fire back.

But without all the hurry and pressure and demands that had existed before.

Together, if he handled things correctly, they could salvage each other.

He wouldn't mess this up.

He envisioned her then, in the shower beside him, soaping down his body while he tongued the sweet hollow of her throat. The imaginary sounds of her pleasure echoed softly in his brain.

Her fantasy touch caused his every nerve ending to sizzle as he pictured her wrapping her arms around him, her wet hair plastered to her face. Those adorably squinchy eyes closed tight, her head thrown back, exposing her vulnerable swanlike neck to his mouth.

His imagination escalated, turning into a rampaging beast, stampeding dangerously out of control.

He mentally brought food into the shower with them. Whipped cream that he squirted on her breasts and then with excruciating slowness licked off. Honey, he dribbled down her belly and cleaned up with his tongue. Her nipples puckered against his lips and she arched her back moaning for more as she threaded her fingers in his hair and tugged demandingly.

"Take me, Beau," he imagined her murmuring.

His erection pulsated so strong he could hardly breathe.

Stop this. Stop fantasizing about her.

But he couldn't.

Under the circumstances, since the cold water wasn't working, there was only one thing he could do.

Steam things up.

Groaning, Beau twisted the faucet toward hot, reached for the bar of soap and lathered up his right hand.

"BEAU?"

Dressed in a pair of Jenny's faded blue jeans that were just a little bit too snug on her and a silky white blouse with long, flowing, bell-shaped sleeves, Marissa pushed into his bedroom, a tray of food clutched in her hands.

She still had on her silver-and-azure four-inch Jimmy Choos, however, as a reminder of who she really was beneath someone else's clothes. She settled the breakfast tray onto the dresser and that's when she heard the sound of the shower running.

''Beau?'' she called again.

She glanced toward the bathroom door; saw that it stood open a few inches. Her pulse tripped when it dawned on her Beau's wet naked body was a mere few steps away.

If she were to sneak over to the door and peer inside, what would she see?

The temptation to snoop was overwhelming.

Don't do it.

He'd known she was returning. He'd left the bedroom door unlocked, the bathroom door ajar…clearly it was an open invitation.

Come.

Marissa Jane, don't you dare.

Compelled by a magnetic force she did not understand but could not deny, Marissa crept toward the bathroom.

Every professional instinct commanded her to leave, but something much more primal urged her forward. Wrong as it was, she longed to catch a glimpse of him naked.

After tiptoeing into the doorway, she craned her neck around the corner.

And gasped.

Oh man, oh man, oh man. The shower glass wasn't frosted and the steamy mist didn't hide much.

Adrenaline pumped through her veins more freely than water through a fire hose. Marissa bit down hard on her index finger at the spectacular sight of pure unadulterated male.

Softly moving into the bathroom, her eyes traced the long hard lines of his torso, the slight curve at the small of his back, his firm, high, round butt.

And his hand, moving.

Her mouth went dry as she realized in one shocked moment what he was doing.

She wasn't naive. She'd watched a dirty movie or two in her life, but she'd never personally witnessed firsthand a man satisfying his needs.

It wasn't right to spy. She was violating his privacy, violating her own code of ethics.

But no matter how hard she tried, she simply could not tear her hypnotized gaze away from his delectable body and his naughty activity. Rooted to the spot, she watched Beau pleasure himself with rising excitement. Her groin grew heavy, burned and ached.

Had he arranged this on purpose? Had he actually wanted her to peek?

The idea that this was a deliberate setup totally singed her flesh. He was enticing her straight into serious jeopardy.

His strokes were long and leisurely. He was in no hurry, completely relaxed, at ease in his own skin. She wished she could be so uninhibited. So blatantly proud of her sex.

He was an inspiring marvel to observe. Long and lean and utterly male. Every feminine molecule in her body responded, contracting into one hard, vibrating knot of yearning.

She wanted him.

More than she'd ever wanted any man.

Until now, she had not truly known the meaning of sexual frustration. At this very moment, what she wanted more than anything else was to strip off her borrowed clothes, kick off her heels, hop into the steamy shower and make it a twosome.

Instead, she simply watched.

A mischievous voyeur, a fetish freak with a penchant for spying, a Peeping Thomasina.

The water slid down his bare back, beaded on his skin. His breathing was labored, his moans of surrender rough and manly.

The intense visual stimulation was too much for her. She couldn't stand it a moment longer. Goose bumps dotted her arms even though her blood was boiling hot. Perspiration pearled in the indention between her nose and upper lip.

This was so wrong but it felt so damn good. She licked her dry lips, mesmerized by what was happening in the shower.

Remarkable.

With his left hand braced against the wall, his right hand working, Beau searched for release.

And she was going insane watching him.

In imitation of his movements, Marissa's own hand

crept to her lower abdomen and her entire pelvis flooded with a sharp, hungry achiness.

Mindlessly, she unsnapped her jeans and slid the zipper down an inch. She slipped her fingers beneath the waistband of both her jeans and her thong panties.

She sought out her warm moistness, awed at how slick and ready she was. Normally it took at least twenty minutes of vigorous foreplay to get her to this point.

Gently, she massaged herself. She could not believe what she was doing. She felt wild and wicked and audacious as hell.

And she didn't want to stop.

Maybe this was a good thing, she argued with herself. Both of them easing their primal needs without complicating their working relationship with sex. The best thing was, he hadn't seen her and he didn't know they were engaged in this tandem but solo performance.

Her secret knowledge shot her arousal into the stratosphere. The water was still running and Beau remained facing away from her. Marissa rested her butt against the sink and lost herself in fantasy.

She imagined it was his hand exploring her body. She felt his big masculine fingers probing the folds of her tender flesh. She gasped when she pictured him slipping his thick middle finger inside her, followed by his ring finger and then slowly sliding his fingers back and forth as his palm caressed the straining nub of her desire.

Her hips undulated with the luxurious fantasy. Excruciating tingles of delight fled down across her body and lodged in the parts of her most feminine.

From the shower stall Beau's breathing grew more shallow, his movements faster.

She matched him pace for pace, her competitive instinct mingling with her sexual desire to produce the most sensual sensation she'd ever experienced.

He was close. So close. She could hear his climax rising in his throat.

And so was hers.

In unison they picked up their tempo for one last push.

She heard him cry out, saw the evidence shoot out from him at the same moment she experienced her own shattering release.

Shimmering cascades of light flashed behind her eyes. Her muscles contracted tight around her fingers. She swayed on her high heels and gripped the counter with one hand as she shuddered against the powerful squeeze of orgasmic sensation.

Stunned, she gasped, desperate to catch her breath. She longed to linger in the haze of the moment but her brain screamed at her.

Get your pants zipped up. Hurry. Get out of here before Beau spots you and realizes what you were doing. Go, go, go.

Heart thumping with excitement and the fear of getting caught, Marissa quickly snapped her jeans closed and slipped back into the bedroom.

Now, if she could only wipe this sly smug grin off her face.

MARISSA WASN'T the only one grinning.

Little did she know Beau kept a small mirror mounted beside the showerhead so he could shave while he bathed. He'd spotted her the minute she'd gingerly poked her head into the bathroom.

He had left the door cracked in open invitation, but he really hadn't expected her to take him up on his subtle offer. She'd delighted him, not only by accepting his covert summons to spy, but by the way she'd kicked the whole event up a hundred notches.

She might be fast-paced and competitive, but the woman was hotter than cayenne pepper and twice as tasty.

Incredible.

Fascinated, he had watched her watching him. Her secret brazenness setting him ablaze.

His guess about her had been correct. Beneath that tough-as-nails-all-business exterior lurked the heart of a true wild child just aching for an excuse to let loose, let go and explore the outer limits of her sexuality.

It had taken an impressive effort of will not to acknowledge her standing there and haul her into the shower with him, Neanderthal style. He was so proud he had controlled his impulses.

Because he had been able to wait, because he had been willing to let her catch him in a very private act, he had gotten the most amazing and unexpected floor show of his life.

Marissa, wildly, hedonistically, taking control of her own sexuality.

That intoxicating image was permanently, indelibly

etched onto his retina. Every time he closed his eyes, he would see her—head thrown back, hair atumble, lips parted, hand busy, busy, busy.

He should have anticipated as much from her. She was a woman who knew what she wanted and went after it, no holds barred. The uninhibited way she'd surrendered to her body stirred him so intimately and intensely he had no words to describe his feelings.

Hot, horny, awed, eager. None of those adjectives even came close to articulating the throbbing swell of emotions growing inside him.

And that's when he'd known that he simply had to have her, no matter the cost. He would pay any price for just one long sumptuous night with the gutsy woman.

That possessive, all-consuming thought had kept his eyes trained on the mirror while he had languidly massaged his granite-hard cock, slowly working them both up into a frenzied crescendo.

He still couldn't believe what she'd done.

Marissa, first watching and then joining in, pleasuring herself right along with him.

He'd never known mutual masturbation could be so stimulating. When she'd unbuttoned her pants and slipped her hand inside the waistband of her jeans, he'd just about come unraveled at the seams.

And the hint of those thong panties peeking out from behind her zipper had driven an arrow of longing through him so intense it literally hurt.

The woman turned him inside out and he knew their little teaser of communal relief wouldn't satisfy either of them for long. Sooner rather than later he was going to have to force her hand and goad her into initiating the first move.

He would have to find a subtle way to seduce her. He'd have to convince her sex play would enhance their work on the video game, not detract from the quality of the product. He simply had to have her and that's all there was to it.

A thousand exotic ideas burst inside his head, a kaleidoscope of earthly physical pleasures.

One way or the other, he would discover her secret sexual desires and use them to win her.

Hmm, what would an aggressive, high-powered, career woman view as the ultimate escape fantasy? His brain clicked and whirled, busy as the computer codes he created.

Would she be into leather and chains? That was pretty aggressive stuff. While Marissa was competitive, he didn't know if she was that edgy in her private life.

Would she like masks and deception and subterfuge? The anonymous-stranger taboo?

Would she get off on danger? Would she like to pretend he was an escaped convict who'd kidnapped her and taken her hostage?

Or was she more into the intriguing concept of an experienced woman tutoring a naive lover and evoking the full extent of his sexual process.

He was getting excited all over again just thinking about the possibilities.

Then an interesting thought occurred to him and he

recognized the truth the moment it popped into his head. Marissa was so hard-driven, so focused on work, so competitive that she probably had no idea what her hidden fantasies even were.

It was his job to unearth her secret desires and use them against her.

But in a very good way.

Beau grinned wickedly at himself in the shower mirror. When she'd commissioned him to design her video game, he was betting Marissa Sturgess had no idea what she was letting herself in for.

A sex game of epic proportions and he wasn't talking about the video software.

He couldn't wait to get started. But for the moment, he had to remain nonchalant about what had happened here in the shower. As difficult as it might be, he had to climb out from under the water, dry himself off, amble back into the bedroom and pretend nothing had ever happened.

Closing his eyes against the red-hot memory, Beau muffled an impatient groan.

Pure torture, this waiting, but he knew time was essential.

He had to let her learn on her own. Slowly, languidly, dreamily. It was his job to create the right environment for her transformation. Lucky for him, Marissa was turning out to be a very apt pupil.

8

BY THE TIME Beau emerged from the bathroom, his body swathed in a thick, blue terry-cloth robe, his beard stubble gone, his gorgeous feet shod in a pair of rubber flip-flops, his damp, dark hair combed back off his face, Marissa had resumed control over herself.

Her laptop was open and running on the desk next to his computer and she had the prospectus from Baxter and Jackson spread out on his bed, which she had hurriedly made.

No point courting temptation.

After what she had done in the bathroom, Marissa had expected to feel awkward and guilty and ashamed. Instead, she felt surprisingly confident and pure and proud.

And that in itself unnerved her.

Her body hummed with vibrant electricity long after her orgasm had subsided, and no matter how hard she tried to stop grinning, she couldn't. To keep Beau from spotting her gloating smile and putting two and two together, she kept her eyes trained on the laptop screen.

Her goal was to keep her thoughts off the mental

image of him in the shower and firmly focused on the task before them.

"Need a hand?" he asked, coming up behind her to touch her on the shoulder.

Her heart thumped. Was it her imagination or had he said "hand" in a very suggestive way?

She was still flustered by what she'd done in the bathroom and terrified that if he had the slightest inkling he would use it against her.

You're just hypersensitive. How could he possibly suspect anything?

"Sit down." She indicated the chair next to her with a brusque wave. "And let's go over the specs for the video game."

"That's not the way I work," he said.

She sighed. "I know. I get the message. You don't work, you play."

He smiled. "Now you're catching on."

She folded her arms over her chest and met his steady gaze. "Okay then," she acquiesced, even though it was killing her to relinquish the decision-making. "How do you suggest we approach the project?"

Beau reached out and gently stroked her hair. Marissa caught her breath at the intimacy of the gesture. She didn't recognize this soft, girlie side of her aching to ooze into a puddle at his feet and beg him to splash around inside her.

"I like the curls, by the way," he said. "Makes you look more relaxed."

"Curls?" She lifted a hand to her bangs.

Oh no, her time in the steamy bathroom must have frizzed her hair. She hopped out of the chair and ran to peer into the bureau mirror.

Blond ringlets encircled her head like a hedonistic halo. A flagrant giveaway that she'd lost control of herself and her emotions.

Damn. Twenty minutes spent on conditioning, moussing and blow-drying her hair shot to shine-ola. She could hear her father's voice in her head. "A messy appearance means a messy mind, Marissa." Desperately, she raked her fingers through her hair in a futile attempt to comb the curls into submission.

"Leave it," Beau said.

While she'd been struggling to tame her hair, he had launched his long body across the middle of the bed and was propping himself up with one arm and noshing on a banana from the breakfast tray she'd brought up.

"I like the new do," he said.

I don't!

The hair made her look like the sort of wanton woman who spied on men in the shower and then pleasured herself. She fought the heated blush that threatened to rise to her cheeks and give away her secret.

"I like the clothes, too," he said. "That silky blouse really enhances your—"

"Look," she interrupted before he could get graphic. "We've got to get started on this project. Why don't you get dressed and finish your breakfast."

"Why don't you come over here." He patted the spot on the bedspread right beside him.

Alarmed, Marissa spun away from the mirror to face him. "I don't think that would be prudent."

"I won't bite," he said. "I promise. That is, unless you want me to."

His bold, saucy wink did serious damage to her resolve.

"I'm comfortable right here, thanks."

"I thought you wanted to get to work."

"I do. So put some clothes on."

He just looked at her.

"Please," she finally added when it appeared as if he wasn't going to budge.

"We're working on a sexy video game. How am I supposed to get into the mood if I'm not feeling sexy?"

"Can't we just sit at the desk like normal people and do this?"

Slowly, he shook his head and patted the bed. "Haven't you figured out by now, I'm anything but normal."

"You can say that again," she muttered.

"If you ask me, you could use a dollop of abnormal in your life."

"I didn't ask you, did I?"

He chuckled.

Don't let him know he's got you on the ropes. If he thinks this doesn't bother you, he'll stop teasing. Just roll with the punches.

Good advice but somehow she couldn't make herself step across the room and join him on the bed.

"Marissa," he whispered in a soft singsong. "I'm waiting."

Sighing so hard her exhaled breath stirred her bangs against her forehead, she tentatively perched on the edge of the bed.

He reached out, grabbed her around the waist and pulled her next to him. Her Jimmy Choos snagged on the bedspread. She felt like a cat digging her claws into the carpet as her owner tried to haul her off to the vet.

"Relax," Beau soothed. "You're as rigid as a park bench."

"I can't relax. I'm in a strange man's bed."

"First time you've ever been in that situation?"

"None of your business."

He grinned. "Feisty. I like that."

"Working. I like that."

"This *is* how I work, Princess. You better just get used to it. Now, lie back against the pillows."

"Beau, I don't…we shouldn't…I thought you said if anything happened between us I would have to initiate it."

"That's right, but this isn't about us. This is about the video game."

She eyed him suspiciously. "You're serious?"

"As the tax man on April 15."

Hesitantly, she leaned back against the headboard.

Beau got off the bed. He was tall and lean and the sight of him dominated her vision as he moved with his loose-limbed amble and disappeared into the bathroom.

"Where are you going?" she asked, feeling a momentary surge of panic.

"Shh." He returned from the bathroom with a bottle of baby oil in his hand.

Oh no. Marissa gulped. This had the earmarks of something very kinky.

He retrieved the chair from behind the writing desk and carried it to the end of the bed. He settled his body into the chair. From her position on the bed, she had a great view of his chest peeping out from the gap in his robe. When his warm fingers wrapped around her right ankle, she squirmed.

"Hey, what are you doing?" She tensed and drew her knee up.

"Helping you to relax." He held out his palm. "Give me your foot."

Grudgingly she lowered her leg.

She hated being in a submissive position, but she had no choice. If she wanted him to work on the project, she had to go along with his stipulations. If she lost the Baxter and Jackson account, not only would she not get the directorship, but she stood a very good chance of losing her job altogether. That was enough to scare her into doing whatever Beau said. He had her over a barrel and, dammit, he seemed to understand the reality of her situation all too well.

He slipped her shoes off and dropped them to the floor one by one. Then he squirted baby lotion in one palm and tenderly began to massage her right foot.

She inhaled sharply at the light tickle of heat seeping up her leg. Until he'd started rubbing her, she had no idea how sore her muscles were or how utterly delicious a foot massage would feel.

"You like?"

Marissa made a low animal noise of pleasure. A half whimper, half growl. It was the only sound she could make. She had lost her voice and misplaced her ability to even form a coherent thought much less string words together. Her mind clung hard to the sensation of his big fingers kneading her eager flesh and refused to focus on anything else.

He circled his thumb against the ball of her foot with increasing pressure. She moaned softly at the resulting ache.

"Hurt?"

She nodded.

"In a good way or bad way?"

"G-good," she stammered.

"Just relax into the massage," he murmured. "That's it. Let go."

In spite of her best intentions to resist his attempts to loosen her up, Marissa found herself melting into the pillows.

"That's it, that's it," he repeated low and somnolent as if trying to put a hyperactive child down for a nap. "Close your eyes."

Her nerve endings tingled, sizzling with blue-white waves of electrical pulses. She soaked up the pleasure, an unwilling but grateful sponge.

"Now," he said. "Now, we can talk business."

"Hmm," she whispered lightly, her mind enshrouded in the beautiful foggy haze of total bliss. "Business."

"Tell me, Marissa, what are your secret fantasies?"

"Excuse me? What did you say?"

"What turns you on?"

She propped one eye open and peered down at him. "Hey, that's kind of personal, don't you think?"

"This video game is all about getting personal. I need a feminine perspective, and if we want this project to speak to Baxter and Jackson's patients, then the scenarios we develop need to spring from something real inside of us. So let's talk about our sexual fantasies."

Marissa thought she would be happy when they'd finally gotten down to work. She was wrong. She was anything but happy. She felt restless and edgy and irritable. She moistened her lips with her tongue. What had she gotten herself into?

"I don't spend much time on sexual fantasies," she said at last. "I'm a busy person."

"That's such a shame."

"What do you mean?"

"Fantasies are the spice of life. I know you have some. Let's dig deep."

"I'd rather not."

"That's because you like deceiving yourself."

"What are you talking about?" She opened both eyes and tried to jerk her foot away, but he held on tight.

"You know. Otherwise you wouldn't be looking so panicky right now. What are you afraid I'm going to find out about you, Marissa?"

"I'm not afraid of you," she denied.

"You're afraid of what I'm going to reveal."

"Is that so?"

He grinned. "Yeah, that's so."

"And where did you get your degree in psychology, Dr. Freud?"

"I've just spent a lot of time thinking about my old life and contemplating my motivations. I recognize the signs. You've been deceiving yourself so long you don't even know you're doing it."

"You're so full of malarkey."

"And you're avoiding the issue. Come on, Marissa. Play with me." He kept caressing her instep with long, feathery strokes. "Tell the truth for once. Deep down inside, how do you like it?"

Marissa shook her head. "I don't know."

"Do you like to be in charge? Or are you secretly longing for surrender?"

She whimpered.

"Ah," he said. "Do you fantasize about a wild-eyed pirate kidnapping you off your Caribbean cruise and whisking you away to his private island. Where he tells you he's seeking revenge against your father and will let you go without harming you but only if you do everything he asks?"

"Maybe," she whispered.

As he spoke, his hand was creeping up past her ankle, gliding over her shin, skimming her knee, fondling the inside of her thigh. Even through the material of her jeans, the sensation was highly arousing.

"Tell me more," he urged. "What else do you like?"

"I can't."

"You can. Do you dream of sex with a stranger? Do you long to be tied up?"

His hand was at her hip now and he was no longer sitting in the chair but on the bed with her, both knees straddling her as he loomed above her. They were face-to-face, their gazes merged.

"Beau, this is insane. I don't feel comfortable talking about this stuff."

"Do you like to play with food?"

"Food?"

In one swift move, he leaned over and reached for the second banana on the breakfast tray.

"What are you doing?"

"Exploring."

"I don't want you to explore."

"Does everything have to be a battle with you? Relax."

He peeled the banana with measured movements and she found she couldn't tear her eyes off his nimble fingers. When he had half the curved yellow fruit exposed, he lowered it to her mouth.

"Taste."

She bit it in two with one swift bite and swallowed it down.

"Ooooh." He grimaced. "Not nice."

GET FREE BOOKS and a FREE MYSTERY GIFT WHEN YOU PLAY THE...

Just scratch off the silver box with a coin. Then check below to see the gifts you get!

SLOT MACHINE GAME!

YES! I have scratched off the silver box. Please send me the 2 FREE books and mystery gift for which I qualify. I understand I am under no obligation to purchase any books, but I will be charged 99p for postage and packing when I receive the FREE book parcel. I am over 18 years of age.

Mrs/Miss/Ms/Mr _____ Initials _____ K6AI

BLOCK CAPITALS PLEASE

Surname _____

Address _____

_____

_____

Postcode _____

7 7 7	Worth TWO FREE BOOKS plus a BONUS Mystery Gift!
🍒 🍒 🍒	Worth TWO FREE BOOKS!
♣ ♣ ♣	Worth ONE FREE BOOK!
🔔 🔔 🍒	TRY AGAIN!

Visit us online at www.millsandboon.co.uk

Offer valid in the U.K. only and is not available to current Reader Service subscribers to this series. Overseas and Eire please write for details. We reserve the right to refuse an application and applicants must be aged 18 years or over. Offer expires 31st March 2006. Terms and prices subject to change without notice. As a result of this application you may receive further offers from carefully selected companies. If you do not wish to share in this opportunity, please write to the Data Manager at the address shown overleaf. Only one application per household.

Mills & Boon® is a registered trademark owned by Harlequin Mills & Boon Limited.

Reader Service™ is being used as a trademark.

The Reader Service™ — Here's how it works:

Accepting the free books places you under no obligation to buy anything but you will be charged 99p for postage and packing for the introductory parcel. You may keep the books and gift and return the despatch note marked 'cancel'. If w do not hear from you, about a month later we'll send you 4 brand new books and invoice you just £3.05*. That's the complete price - there is no extra charge for postage and packing on subsequent parcels. You may cancel at any time, otherwise every month we'll send you 4 more books, which you may either purchase or return to us - the choice is you

*Terms and prices subject to change without notice.

NO STAMP NEEDED!

THE READER SERVICE™
FREE BOOK OFFER
FREEPOST CN81
CROYDON
CR9 3WZ

NO STAMP
NECESSARY
IF POSTED IN
THE U.K. OR N.I.

"What's wrong? You wanted me to pantomime something sexy with your banana?"

"No, although that's not a bad idea. I wanted you to slow down and really experience the taste." He broke off a small piece and trailed it over her lips. "Let's try again."

The light brushing tickled, and a sweet, fruity scent filled her nose. She flicked out her tongue and licked the banana.

When Beau hissed, she realized he was as turned on as she. He trailed the banana down her chin and tracked it over her throat. Her breath came quicker, edgier. He dipped his head to lick off the residue and then stayed at the pulse point in her neck, nibbling and sucking and tasting.

Tormenting her.

Her pulses kicked in unison. In her neck, in her wrist, in her groin. Throb, throb, throb. A heady neediness settled low in her stomach and a ferocious elation unfurled in her heart.

He cupped his hand at the juncture between her legs and massaged her there the same way he'd massaged her feet minutes before. Mindless passion consumed her.

"What are you doing?"

He pulled back and looked down at her. "Marissa," he whispered the name like a prayer. "You're so gorgeous."

"This shouldn't be happening." She hated that her heart soared at his words. "Stop this."

"It's for the game," he said.

"I don't think I believe you anymore. I think it's just an excuse."

"What other foods would you like to play with?" he asked, ignoring her feeble protests.

She couldn't blame him for disregarding her. If she really objected to what he was doing, wouldn't she remove herself from the situation?

"I was taught me not to play with food."

"Forget childhood rules. Jump into the forbidden. Tangling with the taboo is all part of interesting sex play. Do you like sweet and sticky? Honey, caramel, fudge? Or would you prefer tart and tangy? Lemon, barbecue sauce, salsa."

"Neither," she denied weakly.

"Tell me what you like," he coaxed. "If not food play, then what does stoke your engine?"

"Beau…" Her head wanted to tell him to stop but her body was egging her on.

"You can be honest with me."

"I have no secrets to reveal," she fibbed.

"None."

"Not a one."

"Are you sure?"

She shook her head.

"Come on. Admit it." He wagged a finger and grinned. "Are you something of a voyeur, Marissa? Do you get a secret thrill from spying on people?" He lowered his voice. "Do you like to watch?"

HE HAD OVERPLAYED his hand. The minute he'd asked her the voyeur question, Marissa had jumped from the bed so fast she'd knocked him on his can.

She stood before him, eyes wide, palm splayed across her chest, breath seesawing in and out of her lungs. He knew she was disconcerted, but he also knew there was no way on earth she'd admit it.

"I just remembered," she lied through her teeth as she jammed her feet back into her high heels while simultaneously raking her hand through her curls, "I've got to make arrangements to rent the virtual-reality chamber. You stay here and work on the game, I'll drive down to New Orleans and get this taken care of."

"You're not running away from me, are you?" he had asked.

Vehemently, she'd shaken her head, but he'd seen the anxiety in her eyes. He'd gotten under her skin. "No, no, of course not. How long before we'll have the prototype ready to preview?"

"Not for a good month yet."

"Good, good." She was talking fast and inching toward the door. "I'll make the reservations for the end of February."

He'd debated telling her he'd seen her in the bathroom, but decided a head-on confrontation probably wasn't the best route to take. So he had let her escape and he hadn't mistaken the gratitude swimming in her eyes. She knew he knew. That was enough.

In one morning he'd made a lot of progress. With her and with his ideas for the video game.

As he sat at the computer coding in a scripted version of what had transpired in the bathroom, Beau felt a sense of expectation he hadn't experienced in over two years. His pulse was thready. His stomach was tight with excitement. His imagination operating in hyperdrive.

I'm back in the saddle, he thought and an old Arrowsmith song tracked through his brain.

He had to admit the feeling was downright intoxicating. He was damn good at designing games. The question was, how would Marissa act when she realized that he had incorporated their bathroom sexual adventure into the video game's plot?

Smiling to himself, he recalled the taste of her lips, sweet with the flavor of ripe banana. How she'd looked with those steam-induced curls springing adorably around her head, and those gorgeous brown eyes drinking him in. He adored how she smelled of spice and passion and serious determination.

He realized he had stopped typing in midcode and was staring out the window. Mentally, he shook himself. Marissa was supposed to be an inspiration to his creativity, not a hindrance. Not only did he have work to do, he also had the next installment to plan.

Anticipation spurting through his veins, he rubbed his palms together and returned his attention to the computer while one enticing thought echoed in the recesses of his mind.

Where would their game lead them tomorrow?

9

"ARE YOU COMING to the crawfish boil tonight?"
Jenny asked Marissa the next morning. They were
sitting at the formal dining-room table in the parlor,
sharing a delicious sausage-potato casserole and
homemade buttermilk biscuits with six of the B and B's
guests.

Marissa had been concentrating on her food and
struggling to keep her mind off Beau. It was a valiant
battle she'd been fighting—and losing—all night.

The thought that he had seen what she'd done in
the bathroom the morning before sent heated embar-
rassment burning her cheeks. She'd already lingered
too long in the dining room when she should have
been upstairs working on the video game with him,
but she couldn't seem to make herself get up.

"Crawfish boil?" she asked. "What's that?"

"Actually, it's just an excuse for a big party."
Jenny grinned. "The community center holds a crawfish boil one Saturday a month on the town square.
They cook up crawfish and veggies, serve lots of beer,
play zydeco music, and everyone dances until midnight."

"Sounds like fun." Marissa nodded.

Several of the other guests echoed her words and asked Jenny for more details. Marissa sipped her orange juice and let her gaze wander to the big picture window looking out onto the Mississippi River.

A man with a dog strolled into view, and when she realized it was Beau and Anna, she involuntarily caught her breath. She watched him toss Anna a Frisbee a few times. When he bent over to scratch the dog affectionately behind the ear, Marissa found herself tracing the outline of his jeans that molded so provocatively to his bedazzling backside.

He raised his head.

The bright morning sun shone down on him, highlighting his gorgeous profile. The tenderness reflected on his face when he petted the golden retriever caused something strange and indefinable to knot her chest.

"He loves that dog," Jenny said, following Marissa's gaze. "Beau rescued Anna from the pound and she adores him as much as he adores her."

What would it feel like to have such a strong loving attachment aimed at her? As soon as the thought popped into her head, Marissa wished it away. She didn't have the time or inclination for a long-term commitment. She was on the fast track to success, and even if she were to meet a man who wouldn't derail her career, he would certainly have to be a New Yorker who possessed the same values and goals as she. Not some handsome slow-paced Southerner who—while he set her hormones reeling—possessed the irritating talent of pushing all her emotional hot buttons with unerring accuracy.

Beau rose to his feet and flicked his gaze toward the dining-room window. Their eyes met with the vital intensity of lightning striking.

Cocking her his crooked smile, he waved.

Marissa jumped up from her chair. He'd caught her watching him.

Again. She was beginning to wonder if maybe she was a closet voyeur.

He meandered into the dining room just as Marissa was leaving.

"Morning," he greeted her.

"Morning," she mumbled in return.

"Did you sleep well?"

"Fine. Great. Terrific. Never better," she fibbed.

"That's good, because I thought I heard you pacing in your room during the wee hours of the morning, but I must have been mistaken."

"Must have."

He briefly touched her arm. "I hated to think what happened between us disturbed your sleep."

"No, no." She shook her head. "Not in the least."

She stayed firmly rooted to the spot, smiling and lying for all the world to see, when she wanted nothing more than to flee from the intensity of his bemused scrutiny. What was the matter with her? She might be many things, but she wasn't a coward and she never backed away from a challenge.

But the challenge of working side by side with Beau Thibbedeaux was growing more demanding by the minute. By the time this assignment ended, nobody could say she hadn't earned the account direc-torship position.

"Did you get the virtual-reality chamber rented?" he asked.

"Uh-huh." She felt as tongue-tied as she had in high school when she'd been desperate for Mitch Dawson to ask her to the junior prom. That was the last time she recalled being so muddled by a man.

"I'm afraid I let things get out of hand yesterday," he said.

Hand. He said that dangerous word again. Wincing inwardly, Marissa glanced over her shoulder. "Let's not talk about it here."

"I was just going to suggest we find somewhere else to work besides either of our bedrooms."

"Good idea." She nodded vigorously and glanced around the parlor.

One lady sat reading by the fire. Two elderly gentlemen had started a game of chess in the corner by the window. A younger couple sat on the sofa watching a nature program on television.

"I suppose we could work here." She shrugged.

"Too many distractions," Beau said. "We need to concentrate."

"How about the kitchen?"

"The cook is washing breakfast dishes and starting lunch. We'd be in her way."

"Do you have something else in mind?"

"You up for a boat ride?"

"Boat ride?" She made a face.

No one knew of her secret shame, but Marissa

couldn't swim. She was terrified of water. It went back to when she was four and the General had tossed her into the deep end of the pool without preamble and she'd almost drowned.

"I thought it would be a pleasant way to get the creative juices flowing. Nothing helps me think like floating on the Mississippi."

"Isn't it kind of cold? For the boat ride I mean."

"The weather's mild. Sixty-two degrees."

"But won't it be colder on the water?" She curled her fingers into her palms.

"Bundle up in a jacket and it should be okay. But if you'd rather not, we could just suck it up and go back to my bedroom."

She had two choices. The boat or his bedroom? No contest.

"The boat ride sounds fine. Just let me get my jacket."

Ten minutes later they were walking out the back door of the B and B together. Except for the stilettos, Beau's outfit was almost identical to hers—blue jeans, red sweater, black leather jacket. For one eerie minute she felt as if she were staring at her male doppel-gänger.

He led her across the rolling lawn to the small boat-house hunkering at the edge of the river. He undid the padlock and pushed open the side door.

It was dark inside, a smudge of sunlight filtered through the dusty windows and the place reeked with the earthy odor of fish. Four canoes hung on the wall along with a collection of rods and reels and fishing

nets. A speedboat, a pontoon boat and two paddle-
boats bobbed in their slips. Beau pressed a button
beside the light switch, and like a garage door, the
back wall of the boathouse rolled up on a track.

''Ever been on a paddleboat before?'' he asked.

''No.''

Cautiously Marissa picked her away along the narrow plank between the boat slips. Her heels made a
sharp clicking sound as she walked. The weathered
wooden planks were the only things separating her
from the water below. She forced herself not to look
down.

''Take my hand.'' Beau reached across the paddleboat from his plank opposite hers.

Even though she didn't want to, her nervousness
around water pushed her to accept his hand. It was as
warm and inviting as his smile. For a reason she could
not explain, her airway constricted and she found it
hard to draw in a breath. She wobbled on her unstable
shoes.

''Easy,'' he soothed.

She plopped into the paddleboat and let go of his
hand. The minute she did, her breathing returned to
normal. Beau eased down beside her.

''You're going to have trouble paddling in those
heels,'' he commented, staring down at her feet.

''I'll manage.''

Shrugging, he pushed backward on the pedals and
the paddle wheel behind them started churning up water. The raw, earthy scent intensified. Marissa had to
lift her legs to keep from getting whacked in the shins.

''Whoa, whoa.''

He stopped pedaling. ''Put your feet on the pedals.''

Carefully, she placed the balls of her feet on the black rubber pedals.

''We have to play at this together. The only way to power or steer the boat is with our legs.''

''You hate the word *work,* don't you?''

''Pretty well.'' He grinned. ''You ready?''

''As I'll ever be,'' she muttered and tried to dismiss the kernel of fear lodged in her throat.

''Here we go.''

They backpedaled and the boat reversed into the slough.

''Hey,'' she said, ''we're doing it.''

''Having fun?''

She paused a moment, reluctant to admit this new adventure excited her. ''It's okay.''

''I can see fun is a big step for you. I won't push for it. But while we're out here, I don't want you to think about work. I want you to focus on your surroundings. Feel the breeze on your face, inhale the air, hear the river sounds. Get into the spirit of the game.''

''I'll try.''

The day was overcast but still pleasant. Her leather jacket blunted the slight chill. The Mississippi stretched out around them, a wide gray-green ribbon of water.

A sand crane skimmed the river ahead of them, on the lookout for fish. A field stretched out to their right, dotted with big rolls of alfalfa hay. On the left bank, a herd of red-and-white–faced cattle grazed. Other boats navigated the water. A small tug, two fishing boats and, in the far distance, a tour boat.

She liked pedaling the little paddleboat even though her stilettos kept slipping off the damp pedals. It gave her a purpose. Occasionally, she found herself sneaking quick glances over at Beau. There was something surprisingly sensual about watching him. A mantel of rugged naturalist hung on his shoulder and called to her in a very primal way.

''What is it with the shoes?'' he asked after they'd been pedaling in silence for a few minutes, keeping close to the bank.

''They're new. Jimmy Choos. Do you like them?''

''They might be pretty enough in the pages of a magazine, but as real footwear?'' He shook his head. ''I don't see the attraction.''

''Don't they make my legs look long and sexy?'' She fluttered her eyelashes.

''Oh, they do that, all right, but is it worth the torture? Your feet were pretty knotted up when I massaged them yesterday.''

''You get used to walking in high heels. Really, they're pretty comfy,'' she said, just as she felt the beginning of a blister at the back of her heel. Okay, so the shoes weren't exactly made for paddleboating on the Mississippi.

''Ever hear of sneakers? Loafers?''

''Not part of my image.'' She grinned.

''And what image is that?''

"What image do I project?"

"Sharp. Successful. Goal-oriented."

"You got it."

"Overly competitive. Workaholic. A little superficial."

"Now, wait just a minute." She stopped pedaling and glared at him. "Superficial?"

"You asked."

"You really think I'm superficial?"

"Hey, if you wear killer stilettos just so people will think you're hot stuff, I'm sorry, but that's superficial in my book."

His criticism stung. Far more than she would have anticipated.

"It's not superficial," she said in a soft voice.

"Prove it."

"How?"

"Take off those damn shoes before you hurt yourself. You keep slipping off the pedals, and twice you've almost cracked your shins."

"I'm not taking them off."

"Superficial," he teased.

"It's winter, in case you haven't noticed."

"Oh yeah, like those flimsy things are actually keeping your feet warm."

"They're about fashion not warmth."

"You just negated your own argument," he pointed out. "Besides, there's nobody here to appreciate your trendsetting footwear."

"Blast you, Thibbedeaux." She reached down, yanked off the shoes and then carefully tucked them beside her on the seat. Her bare feet felt cool and damp against the rubber and she found the sensation oddly agreeable.

Was she superficial? She didn't feel as if she was superficial. Not in her heart anyway. The shoes meant something to her. Something she couldn't really explain to anyone else.

"Happy now?" she asked.

"Why was that so painful for you? They're just shoes."

"I wear them to prove something to myself."

"Prove what? That you have great legs?"

"Would that be so wrong if I did?"

He eyed her legs cloaked in blue jeans. "You use every tool at your disposal to get ahead, don't you?"

"What if I do?" She notched her chin up at him. She didn't like the way he was evaluating her behavior. "Does that make me a bad person?"

"No. Not at all. In fact, I have to admire the way you see what you want, then go after it with a drive that scares the pants off most people. It's just rather...well...superficial."

"Yeah?" she growled. "Well, I'd rather be superficial than a quitter."

"You calling me a quitter?"

"I heard about the Migosaki deal."

"I suppose you have. I'm told I've become a classic cautionary tale about burning the candle at both ends. But obviously you didn't heed the warning or you wouldn't be here."

"What happened exactly?"

Beau sighed. "I'd accepted too many assignments, tried to juggle too many things at once. Plus, my girl-friend was pressuring me to get married and buy a house in the Hamptons. At the same time I was trying to reconnect with Remy and Jenny."

"But to walk out on a client in the middle of a project…" Marissa shook her head, unable to even imagine it.

"Migosaki was a total perfectionist. He rode my butt 24/7. Called me at home at three in the morning. He had to know every single detail. What can I say? I cracked. Then, when Remy and Jenny reached out and told me to just come home, I did."

The current was swifter here and they didn't have to paddle as hard. The flow carried them along. Greenbrier lay more than a mile behind them now. A fish splashed in the distance but Marissa didn't notice. All her energy was concentrated on the man sitting beside her. His jaw tightened and his hands fisted in his lap.

They were staring into each other's eyes and breathing hard. The air lay charged between them. With passion, with pride, with underlying emotions running swifter even than the river's current.

"But you made a promise. To Migosaki, to your employer."

"So I owe them my soul? You have no right to judge me for leaving."

"And you have no right to call me superficial."

"You're right," Beau said. "I'm sorry."

She wrenched her gaze away from his. She didn't

comment because she was terrified that he was correct. That she was entirely superficial. Her whole life had been built on an iron will to succeed. To prove to her father she was worthy of his love.

Deep down, she feared that if she ever slowed down, she would lose her grip on her dreams. And if she lost her grip on the ultimate prize, then everything she had worked so hard for would slip through her fingers. And if everything slipped through her fingers and she ended up a failure, who would she be then?

A loser her father could never love.

Beau reached over, cupped her chin and forced her face up to meet his gaze. "I truly am sorry. I had no right to call you superficial."

She shrugged off his hand. "Can we go back now?"

"You're right," he confessed. "I am a quitter. I did run away. I couldn't handle the pressure. I hated it when my work stopped being fun, so I stopped working."

"Really, it's none of my business."

"No," he insisted. "You have a right to know what you've gotten yourself into."

You are so much more than I bargained for, she thought.

There was a lot of residual pain reflected in his deep gray eyes, but the minute he realized she had spotted and identified his vulnerability, he laughed and shrugged.

Marissa studied him for a moment and took a wild

guess at the source of his pain. "Your girlfriend, she dumped you when you retired, didn't she?"

"Yeah," he admitted. "But I'm not bitter. Angeline and I simply weren't meant to be."

"How long were you together?"

"Five years."

"That's a long time."

"Generally speaking, I'm a long-term kind of guy," he said.

"Sounds to me like Angeline was the quitter." Marissa was startled to realize she felt like smacking the woman for hurting Beau.

"She's an artist and her career is very important to her. She didn't want kids. I did. It wasn't working on so many levels."

"Well, at least you had a relationship that lasted five years. Not a bad record. Six months is the longest one I've ever had."

He cocked his head and angled her a sideways look. "Why?"

Marissa gazed out at the fields rolling by. "I intimidate most men."

"Yep," he said. "I can see where you might terrify a guy who's insecure about himself."

"I don't scare you, though."

He shook his head. "Hey, I admire your tenacity. I didn't have the guts to stick with the rat race. You're one tough cookie, Marissa Sturgess." He reached over, took her hand and squeezed it.

Not so tough. Right now her heart felt all soft and squishy and vulnerable.

"You don't lack guts, Beau. You just knew what you wanted out of life and it wasn't money. When the love of creating video games disappeared, you were smart enough to get out."

"You brought the love back into my life," he said. "I was resistant at first, but I'm really enjoying working on this game with you. Thank you for being such a pushy dame."

"You're welcome."

Marissa knew he was talking about love of his work, but heaven help her, she wanted him to be talking about the other kind of love. The love of a man for a woman. The kind of love she had never known but always secretly longed for.

A speedboat zipped by them, zigzagging across the water, going too fast. The wake rippled out behind the speedboat.

"Hang on," Beau cautioned. "The wake is going to rock us hard."

Marissa gripped the edge of the tiny paddleboat and the reality hit her all at once. They were out in the middle of the Mississippi River. Somehow, during the course of their intense conversation, they'd forgotten to pedal and drifted far from the shoreline.

Her heart leaped into her throat as the wake hit the paddleboat, jarring them helplessly from side to side. They took on water. It was cold and shocking, running onto the boat, soaking their feet.

Panic skittered through her.

Calm down. Stay focused. In control. Show no fear.

A few seconds later, the rocking waves moved past,

working their way toward the bank. The water ran off and the little paddleboat stabilized.

Marissa breathed easier.

Until she saw her shoe.

One azure-and-silver Jimmy Choo looking Cinderella sad as it bobbed on the surface of the river.

She forgot she was terrified of water. Forgot even that Beau was beside her. Forget everything except the fact her six-hundred-dollar shoe was about to disappear into the murky depths of the Mississippi.

Without stopping to consider what she was doing, Marissa jumped in after the sling back.

10

"BEAU, help me. I can't swim!" Marissa thrashed about in the water.

Her words struck pure terror in Beau's heart. Stupefied, he stared at her. What had happened? Had she slipped? Lost her balance? Fallen?

And then he saw the shoe and he just knew. The crazy woman had gone in after her fashion accessory, never mind she couldn't swim.

Cursing under his breath, he stripped off his leather jacket and dived in after her. The cold water jolted his system and kicked his pulse into overdrive. He shrugged off the initial inertia. Marissa needed him.

His heart pumped harder than a diesel engine and dread weighed him down as he fought the current.

Sputtering and flailing, she went under.

"Stop struggling," he commanded and in two powerful strokes reached her.

When she came up for air, he grabbed her by the collar.

Gasping and coughing, she fought blindly. She grabbed his head and took him under with her.

"Marissa, stop struggling or you'll drown us

both," he shouted when they bobbed back to the surface.

"I can't...I'm scared. Beau, please don't let me drown."

"Trust me," he said. "You have to trust me to rescue you. Just lie back and let me take control."

But his words weren't getting through to her. She kept kicking, splashing, fighting. She attacked the water as she did every problem in her life. Head-on, purposefully, with the full force of her personality. Unfortunately, in this instance, it was exactly the wrong approach.

He pressed his mouth to her ear. "Listen to me, dammit. I'm here. I've got you. Let go. Stop fighting me. I'm not going to lose you."

And then, as if by magic, she went limp in his arms. For one terrifying moment he thought she was unconscious, but when he looked into her face while steadily dog-paddling, he saw she was staring up at him.

"I'm trying," she whispered.

"You're doing fine, Princess. You just relax."

"The water's cold." Her teeth chattered.

"I know. Shh, it's okay."

He held her in the rescue grip he'd learned years ago in first-aid class and swam for shore. They were still a good three hundred yards away and already his muscles cried out with the strain. His body was numb with cold but he didn't allow himself to indulge in a litany of physical discomfort. He had to stay focused or they could both easily drown.

And all for the sake of a stupid shoe.

What was wrong with the woman that those shoes meant more to her than her own life?

Finally, by a supreme effort of will and the strong need to be her savior, Beau defeated the current and pulled them safely to shore. They lay together on the cold, damp, muddy bank, gasping for air.

"What," he growled, after several minutes had passed and their breathing slowly returned to normal, "in the hell did you think you were you doing?"

He glared over at her and that's when he realized she was crying. Her tears hit him like a punch to the gut. Tough, strong, determined Marissa, crying? The sight was almost as shocking as seeing her in the water had been.

His anger—which was really just fear in disguise—melted. He tugged her into his arms and just sat there rocking her. "You scared the life out of me."

"I'm sorry," she whispered, burying her face against his sopping-wet chest and trembling in his arms.

Her skin was ashen, her lips bluish. He had never seen her like this—vulnerable and afraid. Her unexpected weakness tugged at him. For the first time, she had needed him. It made him feel big and strong and protective. A dangerous and scary thing, this feeling.

The earthy scent of her invaded his mind and he marveled at his body's immediate response to their closeness in spite of the circumstances.

"Please," she said. "Don't let me go."

"I won't," he assured her. "I'm here."

Silence settled over them and then she said, "I was so scared, Beau."

"I know, I know. But why did you jump in after that shoe? Especially if you can't swim?"

"They cost six hundred dollars."

"But it's more than just the money."

"Yes."

"What on earth compelled you?" he asked, trying hard to understand.

"I bought those shoes to reward myself. If I signed you, my boss promised me a promotion."

"And that was worth your life?"

"This promotion is something I've been working toward my entire career. Every time I achieve a significant milestone I buy myself a pair of nice shoes."

"So buy another pair and let those sink."

"It was stupid. I know."

"They symbolize more to you than just success. What is it, Marissa?"

She said nothing.

"Well?"

"Whenever my dad sees me wearing new shoes he knows I've done something good."

"And that's a big deal to you?"

She nodded, her wet hair rubbing against his neck. "My father is a brigadier general and very hard to impress."

"And shoes do it for him?"

"Let me try to explain."

"I'm listening."

"My mom died when I was two and it was always

just me and my dad. He was the single most influential person in my life. When I was six and won second prize in the school spelling bee, I came running home with my certificate so certain he would be proud of me." Marissa stopped talking and swallowed hard.

Beau could tell, even twenty years later, the memory still caused her pain. "Let me guess, he wasn't impressed."

"He got a match, set fire to the certificate and made me watch while it burned. Then he told me that second place was for slackers."

And he'd thought Francesca was demanding and hard to live with. He imagined the young Marissa staring at the charred remains of her second-place certificate and his heart wrenched.

"The next year I studied and I studied and I studied and I won that spelling bee. As a reward, the General took me to the shoe store and bought me these red-patent leather Mary Janes I'd been begging for."

"Ah. I'm beginning to understand. That's where your head is at."

"What do you mean?"

"You're still trying to impress a parent. Believe me, I've been there and done that. You'll never be free to follow your own path until you stop trying to be the perfect daughter. Particularly if you have a father who will never give you his full approval."

She swiped away the tears pooling in the corner of her eyes. "Nothing is ever good enough for him. After I won that second spelling bee, he asked me why

I'd made an A minus on my math quiz instead of an A plus.''

He rested his chin against the top of her head, rubbed his hands up and down her arms to warm her. ''Shh, shh. It's all right.''

Her bottom lip trembled and he wanted to kiss her so badly his lips hurt, but he controlled himself. He didn't want her to confuse the complicated emotions following what had happened out there on the river with her real feelings for him. Kissing would only muddy the issue.

Instead, he scooped her up into his arms and started walking.

She did not resist him. Her nonresistance, in and of itself, was amazing. In the aftermath of her near drowning, Marissa had—if at least temporarily—lost her need to compete.

''Where are we going?'' she asked.

''A neighbor's house. They'll give us a ride back to Greenbrier.''

''Okay.'' She wrapped her arms around his neck and rested her head against his shoulder, and for a moment he let himself dream of what could be.

Before Marissa, he'd always been attracted to free-spirited redheads like Angeline and his high-school sweetheart, Cindy. Uncomplicated women with breezy styles and messy, easygoing ways. But somehow, he found himself completely enchanted by this orderly, determined blonde with an impeccable work ethic that concealed the heart of a lonely little girl desperately trying to obtain her father's approval.

She was the total opposite of everything he'd ever thought he wanted in a woman. She was energetic, when he'd thought he wanted relaxed. She was tall and striking, when he'd thought he wanted a dainty, classic beauty. She was a practical businesswoman, when he thought he wanted a dreamy, fun-loving artist.

Marissa tested him in ways he had never considered. She whispered to a part of himself he'd turned his back on. She resurrected his lost creativity.

He found her exciting and optimistic and sexy as hell. He adored that she threw herself into life with a commitment he couldn't fathom. He admired the way she met every challenge unflinchingly.

Most of all, he loved the fact that together they were a harmonious balance of yin and yang, masculine and feminine, light and dark.

Around her, he felt like a hero.

And that was a very perilous thing indeed.

MARISSA HUDDLED under a blanket in the kitchen of the B and B, a space heater directed at her feet. She wore a pair of Jenny's fuzzy red slipper socks.

I could have died, she thought. *And for what? A stupid shoe.*

Worst of all, she could have cost Beau his life, too.

It had been almost an hour since their dunking in the Mississippi and she still couldn't get warm. After changing his clothes, Beau had taken out a motorized skiff to tow in the adrift paddleboat and she was waiting for him to come back, trying out in her head first one apology and then another. Nothing seemed to capture precisely how sorry she was without making her any more susceptible to him than she already was.

Excuse me for being such a bonehead. Forgive me for being the most superficial woman on the face of the earth. Sorry I got your clothes wet, you can send me the dry-cleaning bill. Oops, pardon my faux pas for almost getting you drowned.

He had every right to be furious with her. She'd deserved a thorough bawling out. Instead, he had been kind and calm and understanding. His good-natured patience made her feel much worse than if he'd yelled at her.

The General would have yelled at her. Marissa cringed at the very thought.

Jenny had brewed her a cup of herbal tea and she sat across the table staring at her with inquisitive eyes, waiting for the details Marissa was too ashamed to give.

"You okay?" Jenny asked.

"Don't be nice to me. I don't deserve it."

"Oh, please." Jenny rolled her eyes. "So you made a mistake. You're okay. Beau is okay. That's all that matters."

"I feel like the world's biggest idiot."

"You're not. Believe me, we've all pulled silly stunts we regret. In high school, I streaked through the crowded lunchroom on a dare."

"You?"

"I'm not as sweet as I look." Jenny winked. "It wouldn't have been such a disaster except I slipped on a glob of Jell-O, went sliding across the floor and came to a stop right at the principal's feet."

"Impressive." Marissa couldn't help giggling at the image.

"Don't laugh. Do you have any idea how much detention you can get for an infraction like that?"

"I'm guessing a lot."

"Try half a semester. See, jumping into the river after your shoe doesn't look so impulsive now, does it?" Jenny smiled.

"Thanks for cheering me up."

"Pah." She waved a hand.

A bell rang in the lobby. Jenny got up. "Sounds like I've got guests. You stay here and sip your tea. We can talk more later if you want."

"That would be nice." Marissa returned her smile. Jenny was such a wonderful person. She wondered why she didn't have more female friends back home.

Probably because you're so focused on climbing the next rung of the ladder. You've never really had time for cultivating close friendships.

Sad but true.

Marissa took a sip of the cinnamon-scented tea and savored the heat slipping down her throat. Today had been something of a turning point for her in more ways than one. For the first time in her life, she'd had it graphically illustrated to her exactly how much her father's influence ran her life. She was twenty-six years old and she still allowed his disapproval to dictate her behavior.

To the point of jumping into a cold river in order to rescue a symbol of her success.

Crazy. Illogical. Embarrassing. But she'd done it.

Something had to change.

How could she stop letting her father's expectations drive her?

You could start by realizing you don't have to be perfect.

Marissa gulped. For her, it was a radical concept. She'd been raised to believe that perfection was the only goal. To suddenly discard a lifetime of indoctrination seemed impossible. For whatever reason, she was who she was.

You can change.

But could she? Really?

What would it take to start untying the shackles of her past?

The words Beau had been repeating to her from the moment they'd met floated into her head.

Relax. Let go. Have fun. Surrender.

Ah jeez. It sounded so nice and yet so impossible. Where on earth did she start?

And then Beau stepped through the door, the surviving Jimmy Choo in his hand, that sexy grin on his face and all at once, she knew the answer.

THE CRAWFISH BOIL was in full swing when Beau, Marissa, Jenny and a handful of Greenbrier's guests pulled the B and B's courtesy van into the parking lot on the south side of the square. Beau sat behind the wheel. Marissa rode shotgun. Everyone else was packed into the back.

Marissa had finally gotten warm. She wore green woolen slacks, a mauve sweater and a pair of Jenny's sneakers. It felt weird being out of her high heels and the sneakers didn't match with her outfit, but she didn't care. She wasn't herself. Which was a good thing. She'd decided for the duration of her stay in Louisiana she was going to be someone different.

Beau took her hand and they walked across the parking lot together. The sight before them played out like a scene straight from *The Big Easy*.

A dozen large washtubs boiled on propane cookers under tent awnings. Long community tables, covered with newspaper and surrounded by folding chairs, stretched in long rows across the courthouse lawn. The night was alive with sounds of accordions and harmonicas running the scales and guitars tuning.

The aroma of garlic, peppers and onion drifted on the air. Children ran laughing and playing tag between the legs of chatting adults. Outdoor party lights were strung from the cypress trees. All around her, people spoke with the lazy Cajun lilt she was swiftly growing to love.

"Would you like a beer?" Beau asked.

Normally, she didn't drink beer but she'd made a vow to herself. Try new things. Experiment. Go out on a limb. "Sure."

They stood in line for their turn at the tapped keg. Beau filled a plastic cup with the frosty rich amber brew and passed it to her. Marissa took a sip.

''Uncle Beau, Uncle Beau.'' A pretty little dark-haired girl ran from the crowd to wrap her arms around Beau's waist. A smaller boy, who possessed the same dark hair and rapid-fire dimples as the girl, flanked her.

Beau hugged both children, then turned to Marissa. ''Marissa, meet my niece and nephew, Sarah and Willis.''

''Hi.'' Marissa smiled at them.

''Is this your girlfriend?'' Sarah asked.

Beau's gaze meet Marissa's. ''We're friends, yes.''

Willis eyed her for a moment. ''You're not so yucky.''

Marissa lifted a bemused eyebrow. ''Why, thank you.''

Beau laughed and shook his head. ''Don't ask what that's all about.''

''I'm assuming he's at the girls-have-cooties stage.''

''You've got it.''

''Remember me?'' Beau's brother, Remy, greeted her with an easy smile identical to Beau's and a casual handshake.

''From the bar on Bourbon Street. Of course.''

''This is my wife, Allie.'' Remy slipped an arm around the waist of the dark-haired, compact woman standing beside him.

Allie Thibbedeaux looked just right for a festive evening in Fleur de Luna, Louisiana. She had on a long-sleeved yellow-flowered shirtdress with a white button-down sweater thrown over her shoulders and a simple gold locket around her neck.

She embraced Marissa in a warm hug. She smelled invitingly of lavender and crayons. "Welcome to our little corner of the world." Her eyes were sharp and lively. "Hope you like crawfish."

"I've never had it before," Marissa confessed.

Remy shot Beau a mischievous glance. "You gonna teach her how to suck the head?"

"Remy Thibbedeaux." Allie nudged her husband in the ribs. "You behave yourself."

"Ah, *chère*, what's the fun in that?" Remy lightly goosed Allie's bottom and she jumped, giggling. The way his face lit up when he looked at his wife caused a wistful stirring deep inside Marissa. Would she ever have that kind of loving relationship with a man?

Unbidden, her gaze wandered to Beau. He was standing back a bit, watching her.

Her heart gave a crazy little bump.

The musicians had finished tuning up their instruments and were now deep into the bluesy music.

"Care to dance?" He extended his hand and smiled at her. But it wasn't his usual lopsided, playful grin. This smile was hotter, more sensual and promised all the sex that she could handle.

"I'd love to."

He took her cup of beer and set it down on a table along with his own. Then he swept her into his arms and swung her out onto the concrete slab that passed for a dance floor nestled in the midst of the cypress trees.

Marissa wondered if everyone in the town square could feel the heat sizzling between them the way she could. She'd never felt so attuned to her body. All her five senses were honed to a razor point.

The beer taste lingering in her mouth was tart and yeasty. A piquant scent of his decadent aftershave evoked memories of her mother's spice cabinet. The feel of his crisp starched shirt appealed to her sense of order. The jangly vibrations of the exotic zydeco music rolled through her ears. And the sight of Beau's silver-gray eyes captivated like nothing else could.

She was going to do it. Take the plunge and succumb. She wanted him. Wanted this wild, crazy, headlong feeling to stretch into infinity.

The prickly awareness of just how fleeting their affair would be imparted a bittersweet intensity. She was beginning to understand Beau's penchant for slowing things down, taking his time.

For Marissa time had always been a commodity, something she could negotiate, manipulate, use to her advantage. She wasn't one to squander it. But what she'd once seen as wasting time suddenly shifted and changed.

They danced in the twinkling light. The melody was a low, soft wistful refrain that spoke longingly of lost love.

A lump clogged her throat as Beau held her close. He softly crooned the Cajun song like a lullaby.

Bubbles of contentment mixed with a sweet impossible yearning rose to the surface and then popped with a bright intensity. Bliss. Sadness. Delight. Melancholia. Pop, pop, pop went her emotions.

Like champagne. Fizzy. Delicious. Heady. Dizzy.

But would she wake tomorrow with a horrible hangover, full of regrets for surrendering to the moment?

She pushed aside the notion and immersed herself in her environment. She noticed everything, memorized every nuance, every sight, sound, smell. The closeness of other couples dancing around them, clutched tight in the embrace of lovers. The casual brushing of Beau's sleeve against her neck. His fingers trailing over her bare flesh. She loved the tension in the air. Loved how alive and tingly his touch made her feel.

The power of Beau's body heat radiated through her sweater and into her chest, inundating her with his masculine essence. When he pressed his forehead against hers and stared deeply into her eyes, her heart puddled, liquid as hot candle wax.

Her body urged to merge with him, even though this was a world where she did not fit. Call it a sidestep. A sensualized, exciting trip to a foreign land. Here, none of the rules from her land applied. Was that the fascination?

She felt as if an unexpected door had opened. Until coming to Louisiana her life had been precision, programmed and plotted. One goal leading to the next and then the next and then the one after that, plodding forward in an endless series.

In this dreamy, languid, delicious world, she experienced a sense of liberation, of possibility, and she squeezed it with her entire heart.

If just for the moment.

Beau two-stepped her over the rough concrete floor, the scent of him driving her straight over the edge of reason. His masterful hands caressed her waist, the small of her back. Little by little his intriguing fingers slid down her spine until he was cupping her derriere in both hands. His wicked hotness burned her wherever he touched and consumed her with yearning. Marissa shuddered against him.

She realized they hadn't spoken once during the course of their dance. They let their bodies do the talking.

She felt him harden against her. Closing her eyes briefly, she whimpered. Now was the time. He was ready, she was receptive. She had to act before she changed her mind.

"Beau," she whispered.

"Marissa." The sound was a caress.

"You told me that if anything happened between us that I would have to initiate it."

"What are you saying?" He stopped dancing. Stopped moving altogether. Other couples bumped off them but they didn't really notice. They were staring deeply into each other's eyes.

Both hoping, wishing, wanting.

"I'm initiating it. Take me home. Take me to bed. Make love to me."

"Are you sure this is what you want?"

"More than anything."

"Why?"

"Does it matter?"

Oh gosh. Would he actually turn her down? The thought had never occurred to her.

"I don't want you doing this for all the wrong reasons," he said.

"What would be the wrong reasons?"

"Because you're feeling vulnerable about what happened on the river this morning. Because you're using sex as an apology. Because your real world is very far away and you're feeling lonely or confused or bored. Because you're thinking sex will solve any of your problems."

"And what would be the right reasons?"

He swallowed so hard his Adam's apple strained against his throat. "Because you simply want to have fun and enjoy yourself. Because you want to seize the moment. Because you want to be some way, someone *you've* always wanted to be. Because you're attracted to me and I'm attracted to you and we can see in each other what we lack in ourselves."

He ran a hand up and down her arm, his gaze searching hers, trying to read her intent.

"Those are my reasons."

"You're certain? I don't want to end up as your deepest regret."

It took a lot for her to ask for help. Pleading went against her competitive nature. But he'd made it clear he was putting on the brakes if she couldn't convince him this was really what she wanted.

"Beau," she pleaded with her eyes, telegraphing to him exactly how sincere she was. "Please, show me. Teach me. I want to learn how to have fun in bed."

11

THE PRESSURE WAS ON. Marissa wanted him to teach her how to have fun in bed. He had his work cut out for him, limbering up his gorgeous New Yorker. More importantly, would he be able to live up to her high expectations?

Beau realized he was nervous. Damn nervous. So nervous he was grateful when the music stopped, the dinner bell clanged and the mayor hollered, "Crawfish is on."

"Could we just skip dinner?" Marissa asked. "And head back to Greenbrier?"

"A good seduction starts slowly. And food is an excellent first course." Beau took her hand and led her off the dance floor. "I know you have a tendency to cut to the chase, but the buildup is half the fun. Come on."

They joined the gathered crowd, watching while the cooks drained the water from the washtubs, and with the appropriate ceremony dumped the contents out onto the picnic tables.

No matter how many times he saw it, the hodge-podge of sights and aroma never failed to evoke in him a sense of childish delight. Orange-red crawfish sprawled in a pile over the black-and-white newspaper along with yellow ears of corn, sliced purple onions, green bell peppers, pink new potatoes and thick andouille sausage.

Beau eyed Marissa's expensive sweater. "Let's get you a bib."

"Oh, that sounds terribly sexy."

"Eating mudbugs is messy."

"Mudbugs?" A worried little frown creased her forehead.

"Another name for crawfish."

"Eeew."

"Don't be alarmed," he said, guiding her over to where the cooks were passing out plastic bibs, paper napkins and packages of saltines. "You've eaten lobster right?"

"Uh-huh."

"Same general idea except they're smaller and spicier." He moved to tie the bib on for her. She lifted her hair to get it out of the way. His fingers grazed the bare skin at the nape of her neck. The contact was slight, but powerful enough to send his heart careening into his rib cage.

Unprepared for the blitz of his reaction, Beau stepped away from her. She turned to face him and her happy grin was almost his undoing

"Have a seat." He pulled out two chairs at the nearest table. "I'll go grab us a couple more beers to wash this down with."

"Where do we get plates?"

"No plates."

"No plates?"

Beau shook his head and then nodded at their tablemates picking through the food with their fingers. "Dive right in."

When he returned with their beers, he found her tentatively eyeing a crawfish.

"Okay," she said. "I'm ready to give it a try. How do we start?"

"Make sure its tail is curled." He sat next to her. "A straight tail means he was dead before cooking and might not be so good to eat."

"They boil them alive?" She looked stricken.

"As a competitor, you know well enough it's a rough world."

"Eat or be eaten, huh?"

He smiled.

She let out her breath and reached for a plump, curly-tailed crawfish. "Now what?"

"Hold the mudbug like this and grasp on to a claw. Pull it up and down until it snaps off."

Gamely, Marissa did as he directed, doing the same with the second claw. Beau picked up a crawfish of his own and mimicked her procedure.

"Put a claw between your teeth like this." He demonstrated.

She followed suit and he was treated to a tantalizing glimpse of her pretty pink tongue. His entire body tensed at the provocative sight.

"Like this?" Her words were slightly garbled as she spoke around the claw.

"Uh-huh." He was so mesmerized by her mouth he couldn't focus on anything else.

His mind reeled with the possibilities of what those luscious lips might be doing to him later on in the evening. Captivated, he didn't realize a long moment had passed.

"And?" she said.

"Uh…yeah…crack it open and suck out the meat."

Shyly at first, she slowly probed the claw with her tongue. "Oh!" Her eyes brightened. "It's delicious."

After she eagerly fished the meat from the second claw, he showed her how to flip the tail over, soft side up and split, crack and peel away the first two rings of the shell surrounding the tail and extract the meat hidden there.

She discarded the spent crawfish carcass in the bucket provided for that purpose and tore into another one.

Her obvious enjoyment of the exotic food did strange things to Beau. She was willing to try new things, and once fully embarked on her journey attacked the experience with gusto that spoke well for what was to come later.

Watching her lips sent his mind back to the first moment he'd seen her walk into Remy's bar. If someone had told him five days ago he'd be sitting here at a messy crawfish boil with that methodical uptight urbanite, he wouldn't have believed it for a moment.

He'd underestimated her. She was more adaptable then he'd given her credit for. She was certainly more adaptable than he was. She was doing great down here in the Louisiana bayou, whereas he'd been a miserable failure in New York.

His admiration for her grew by staggering proportions.

She swallowed a big gulp of beer, stuck out her tongue and fanned it. "Spicy hot."

"That's Cajun cuisine."

"But I love the flavors. It's a mad jumble of taste sensations. Blazing cayenne, tangy lemon, rich bay leaf, pungent garlic, minty thyme. Yum."

"I'm glad to see you're enjoying the meal."

"You're not eating. What's wrong?" She paused to dab her mouth with a napkin.

I'm saving my appetite for other things, he thought wickedly but said, "I'm having too much fun watching you go at it"

"Here." She reached over, plucked up a potato wedge and extended it toward him. "Have a spud. They're great too. Buttery and sweet."

He wrapped his tongue around the potato, purposefully licking the tip of her finger in the process. Marissa sucked in her breath and the sound hit him hard and low. She kept feeding him and each time he boldly licked her fingers.

"Oh, my." She exhaled.

"We better save room for dessert," he said when she offered him a slice of sausage. "I heard they're serving bourbon-pecan brownies."

Her soft moan of pleasure was a stake right to his groin. "Can we get them to go?"

"I'm liking the way your mind works."

She wiped off her hands, quaffed the rest of her beer and hopped to her feet. Her cheeks were pink, her brown eyes sparkling with excitement. "Let's get out of here."

Her excitement fueled his own. "I'm right behind you, Marissa. All the way."

THEY LEFT the van keys with Jenny and walked the half mile back to Greenbrier, holding hands and giggling like teenagers. Marissa was woozy-happy from the beer and Beau's proximity. The smell of his zest made her feel giddy and glad.

The wind rustled the cypress trees and ruffled his dark hair. She couldn't stop glancing over at him, admiring the way the silky strands curled around his collar.

Her skin prickled, hypersensitive. Her body was sore with ache, hungering for his touch. How had she come to be here? So desperate for this man. On the verge of something remarkable and yet utterly temporary.

He led her up the front-porch steps and into the empty foyer. Their footsteps echoed against the hardwood floor. He pulled her into his arms and pressed his mouth to hers as if he wanted to eat her whole. Her reaction was intense and immediate. An inferno galloped through her body and she converged his fervor with her own. He kissed her openmouthed, his tongue uncompromisingly fierce.

Where had her slow, laid-back Southern man gone?

His wide palms cupped her bottom and he lifted her feet off the ground. Crazed, Marissa wrapped her legs around his waist, felt the dull poke of his belt buckle against the inside of her thigh. Turning with her in his arms, he positioned her with her back pressed into the wall. His erection, hard and thick, pulsed against her.

She was ready to rip open the front of his shirt with her teeth, but she forced herself to let him hold the reins. She didn't want him accusing her of going at their lovemaking as if it were a corporate takeover.

His arousal fired hers higher, thrusting her to the very limits of her control. Provoked, she moaned and crushed him tighter between her thighs.

Swearing softly under his breath, he gentled his grip on her fanny and lowered her to the floor. "I'm sorry. I'm rushing this. Not here. Not yet. It's just that you've got me so fired up I can't think straight."

She slumped her forehead against his chest and he threaded his fingers through her hair. He smelled so good. Like life itself. Closing her eyes, she fought hard to bring her libido under control.

"Look at me."

She raised her head, opened her eyes.

"There." He smiled. "I had to make sure you were all right."

"I'm fine," she lied.

She was anything but fine, she was on fire for him, ablaze with need, broiling with lust, and the only thing that was going to extinguish her desire was to take his body inside hers.

Grasping both her hands in his, Beau faced her and walked backward to the staircase. Slowly, deliberately, never taking his eyes off hers, he moved up the steps one at a time until Marissa despaired that they would never reach the top.

When they finally got to the landing, Beau let her go and opened his bedroom door, then he fetched one of the rocking chairs from the hallway, dragged it over the threshold and positioned it at the foot of the bed.

"What's that for?" she asked from the hallway.

"Wait and see."

Her curiosity piqued, she followed him into the bedroom.

He shut the door behind them. "Come here."

Marissa slipped into his arms with surprising ease. She wasn't accustomed to sexual relationships feeling so effortless, so uncomplicated, so right. She fit perfectly into the curve of his elbow.

He rested his chin against her head and slipped his hand up under her sweater. Her ear was pressed to his chest and she could hear the staccato thumpity, thump, thump of his heart eerily matching her own fretful rhythm.

He stroked her hair with one hand while caressing her bare midriff with the pad of his other thumb. "Are you still sure this is what you want?"

"Absolutely."

"I don't want you to compromise your principles. It's not too late to change your mind."

She was walking into this with her eyes wide open.

She wasn't expecting anything more than a good time. That was all she wanted.

Or so she told herself.

"I'm a big girl. I know what I'm doing. Just shut up and kiss me."

"Yes, ma'am."

"I've got condoms." She reached into the front pocket of her slacks and drew out two.

"And just in case those aren't enough." He extracted three from his wallet and grinned.

"Five times in one night?"

"You never know." He cupped her jaw in his palm, tipped her chin up and kissed her. Quieter, softer, calmer than he'd kissed her just moments ago in the foyer.

The brush of his lips against hers sent a flood of moist heat throughout her body. Every cell of her being throbbed with raw awareness, until she was a spinning field of vibrating energy. She opened to him. A flower to the rain.

Beau slid the tip of his tongue between her teeth and she exalted at the intimacy of inviting him inside her body. Twining her arms around his neck, she pressed back against his tongue with her own. The hem of her sweater rode up, exposing a strip of flesh to the air and he splayed his palm just above the area, right at the nip of her waist.

Sinking her fingers into his forearm, she tilted her head and took his tongue ever deeper into her mouth. A minute passed, when she was conscious of nothing but his heat and taste and sheer masculine presence.

Then another minute and another. Her lungs burned, but it was such a sweet, glorious ache she never wanted it to stop.

Finally, she had to breathe. Gasping, she broke her lips from his.

''Beau,'' she whispered. ''Beau.''

''Yes, sweetheart?''

''Nothing. I just wanted to say your name.''

She clung to his neck, arched her pubic bone against his pelvis, thrilled to the rock-hard erection hidden beneath his jeans.

He groaned. ''You vicious minx. If you don't ease off the teasing, our first time is going to be over before we even get started.''

''Premature ejaculator, are you?'' she joked.

''Not usually, but you, Princess, could make a dead man come.'' He ran his thumb along her navel.

It tickled and she squirmed.

''It's been a while for me,'' he confessed.

''Looks like you just got lucky.'' She pressed a finger to his chin.

''Looks like.''

Boldly, she cupped the fly of his zipper with one hand, while at the same time lightly biting down on his bottom lip.

''Stop toying with me, woman,'' he growled.

''Who's toying? I'm deadly serious.''

The minute she said the words, she realized she was up to her old tricks. Moving fast, taking control, making sex a competition.

Ack!

Blinking, she stepped away from him. She had no clue how to take it easy, let go of the reins, stop reaching so hard for the ultimate goal.

"Marissa?" He was studying her face closely. "What's the matter?"

She sank onto the bed and hugged herself. He sat next to her.

"Did I do something wrong?" he asked. "Did I say the wrong thing?"

"It's not you." She shook her head. "It's me."

"I'm listening."

She told him then. About Steve and her other lovers. How she'd never been able to relinquish control in the bedroom. "I can't stop making everything a contest. Not even sex."

"You just need practice," he murmured and nuzzled her neck. "I've got an idea."

"Oh?" She perked up. "I'm open to suggestions."

"I propose a role-playing game."

"Tell me more."

"Let's pretend you're a virgin. You were raised in a convent and you've never seen a naked man before. You're shy and innocent and trusting."

"Oooh, I like this game. Who are you?"

"I'm a noble knight. Your convent has been burned to the ground. I find you wandering the countryside, alone and in imminent danger. You've turned to me for help."

Tingles raced up her spine as he detailed his sinful scenario. "Yes, yes, go on."

"I've taken you to an inn."

"Must we share this room, kind knight?" Marissa asked, slipping into her role of wide-eyed virgin. "I fear for my reputation."

"Dear lady," he said, "it's the last room at the inn. The hour is late. No one need know we are together."

"But the innkeeper..."

"A friend who will remain silent."

Their eyes met and Marissa found herself transported into the fantasy they were creating.

"But sir, we are strangers. Are we both to sleep in this bed?"

"No, fair lady, I shall sleep on the floor."

"Oh no, gallant sir, I cannot allow you to sleep on the cold stone. You saved my life. I insist you take the bed and I'll sleep on the floor."

"No man worthy of calling himself a knight would allow a lady to sleep on the floor while he takes the bed."

"That settles it then," she said. "We share the bed." Marissa sat there, not sure what to do next. Her instinct was to throw him onto the covers, whisk off their clothes and jump his bones. She fisted her hands and dropped them into her lap to keep herself from doing just that and waited.

And waited.

Tentatively, she peeked over at him.

He was watching her intently, his darkened eyes steeped with hungry need.

She gasped. "Sir, why are you looking at me like that?"

"You are chaste, maiden, and I am but a man, weak with desire for you. I don't dare tempt the fates by sleeping in the same bed with you."

"Not even if I wanted to repay your kindness with my virtue."

"My lady, the price is too high to pay. It would be wrong of me to take advantage of you."

Take advantage of me, Marissa wanted to scream, but she knew they were playing this game for a reason. She needed to learn to appreciate a slow seduction.

"But you selflessly risked your life to save mine. I want to give you my most treasured gift."

"Oh, maiden," he breathed. "Don't tease."

Marissa got to her feet, startled and thrilled to find she was trembling as if she really was a convent girl confronted with the prospect of offering her virginity as a reward to the gallant knight who was protecting her. She found the idea highly sexual and wondered why she had never explored this particular fantasy before.

"I'm not teasing, kind knight. I am yours for the taking." In increments, she grasped the hem of her sweater in both hands and slowly inched it up over her head and let it drop to the floor.

Beau sucked in his breath. "My lady, you are too beautiful to bestow your favors on this humble servant."

Fingers shaking, heart pounding, she undid the button on her slacks. Once she was naked except for her panties, she timidly approached him.

"I've always been curious about what it felt like to lie with a man. Teach me." She reached out a hand to him. "Show me how to please you."

"Lie down beside me," he whispered, stretching out his body on the bed and patting the covers next to him.

Breathlessly, she obeyed.

"Now close your eyes."

She did.

He pulled the sheet up to her neck.

Her body taut with anticipation, her eyes tightly closed, Marissa waited.

With the gentlest, barest hint of a touch, his fingers whispered over the pounding pulse point at her throat. In her experience, most men rubbed a woman's body too roughly, anxious to get the feel of her. But not Beau. He seemed to know exactly what she needed, as if this game was strictly for her pleasure alone.

What an unselfish lover!

Her mounting anticipation intensified. Static electricity from the combination of his hands, the sheet and her fine body hairs created a mind-bending sensation so subtle and yet so rich.

He skimmed three fingers over her face, tenderly tracing the outline of her forehead, floating above the crevices of her eyes, the straight line of her nose, the curve of her ears and on down the column of her neck.

With an incredibly slow motion, his fingers dipped and glided over her bare flesh. Using the flat of his hand, he hovered above her, moving from her neck to her feet, and created a powerful connection out of their combined energies.

He continued the airy massage for a good ten or fifteen minutes, never speaking, never touching her firmly. He had her flip over onto her stomach and did the same slow, sensual caress to her back. Sliding from the top of her head, down the nape of her neck to her shoulders. His fingers danced over her spine to the small of her back, to her buttocks, her calves, her ankles.

Her muscles tensed with excitement. Her heart skipped and thudded with the nerve-wracking stimulation. Whenever he found an erogenous zone that made her moan, he would linger.

At the tender area of her inner arm, at the juncture between her buttocks and her upper thighs, underneath her jaw, along her navel.

She twisted and squirmed, keeping her eyes shut, savoring the mounting pleasure.

His heated hands sculpted to each soft curve of her body. He gently turned her over again and when he reached the waistband of her panties, he slowly slipped his hand inside to find the warm mound of her womanhood.

He used his palm to massage the entire outer area with slow, circular motions. Then with the heel of his hand, he lightly pressed into her center, delicately using two fingers to stroke from the top of her hooded treasure to the moist entrance of her very womanly essence.

She whimpered, arched her back and fisted the sheets in her hands.

"I want to give you a special treat, maiden, to repay the fine gift you have given me."

"Yes, knight?"

"Kneel on the bed."

Alive with lust and thrust and exhilaration, Marissa knelt before him, bracing herself on her elbows and burying her face into the pillow.

What was he going to do?

The suspense of not knowing was driving her completely insane.

He knelt behind her. When his bare legs brushed against hers, she realized for the first time he was naked too and her excitement skyrocketed.

"Your thighs are so beautiful. I am a most fortunate knight to have rescued such a generous lady," he said in a soft voice, and rubbed her fanny. "And you are perfect in every way."

Omigosh. She could not breathe. Didn't want to breathe. Breathing interfered with her concentration on what was happening behind her.

"I love your panties. White cotton innocence but naughty, naughty thongs."

She didn't know if they were still playing chivalrous knight and willing virgin but she didn't care. When he caressed the fabric of her panties, pulling on her thong until it rubbed against the hood of her most tender spot, she almost came right then and there.

Beau planted white-hot kisses along her cheeks and

then tugged her panties down, his heated breath blistering her bare skin. He slipped his hands between her tender folds and stroked her there, too. His fingers were silky wet with liquid and she caught the scent of strawberry massage oil.

Gently, his inquisitive fingertips explored between her thighs, parting the petals of her feminine flower. And then he slipped his thick middle finger into her, sliding in and out, in and out until she thought she would simply go mad.

He added his ring finger into the fray while his glorious pinkie slid forward to caress her exquisitely tender spot. His wrist rocked back and forth to a slow, steady beat, easing his two middle fingers in—no more than an inch—and then out again, all the while his pinkie circled, round and round, picking up speed and thoroughly glazing her with the glossy massage oil.

Marissa whimpered and groaned and begged for him to stop playing torturous mind games. She cried out for him to thrust into her, but Beau was ruthless in his chivalry and he would not take his pleasure until she had hers.

And then he did something that went beyond all previous sensations. With his smooth wet index finger, he began to rim the tight puckered rosebud of her bottom. Touching it, pressing against it with firm yet light pressure.

The rhythmic pressure was astounding. Then he oh-so-gently, oh-so-softly squeezed his fingertip into her tight entrance. He pumped his hand, back and forth, following the sway of her hips. He picked up the pace but remained gentle in the process, babying her aching flesh.

His middle finger moved deeper, faster, exploring her G-spot. His little finger flicked wildly across her swollen wet flesh.

"Beau," she cried out his name and thrashed against him. "Beau, Beau, Beau."

She rode his hand, pushing and pulling, rocking and bucking.

And then, in an explosion of pure rhapsody, she came. Her muscles tightened. Her pulse pounded. She saw the yellow-white burst of a million stars behind her shuttered eyelids and her wet heat poured from her, flowing out onto his palm.

Chuckling softly, Beau removed his hand and she collapsed onto the bed, gasping blindly for breath.

"That was, that was, that was," Marissa repeated, unable to complete the sentence, unable to complete her thought.

"Not over," he said.

The next thing she knew, he had her by the ankles and was pulling her toward the end of the bed.

12

BEAU SANK INTO the armless rocking chair, hauling Marissa down with him as he went. He cradled her against his chest, allowing her to catch her breath before he started again. Her husky little gasps filled the steamy room and he found the soft sound oddly endearing.

With the pad of her thumb, she stroked the contours of his chest muscles, a lazy smile on her face.

"Hmm." She sighed and her eyes closed. "Hmm."

"You going to sleep on me?"

She cracked one eye open. "Not on your life. I'm just savoring the moment."

"Good for you," he said. He had a suspicion Marissa rarely savored the present moment and he was glad to see her seizing it now.

Because now was all they had. No future existed for this relationship beyond the completion of their video game.

A sudden bittersweet wistfulness swept over him, but he banished the feeling before it had time to sprout and grow. He'd gone into this affair with his eyes wide open. He refused to have any regrets.

She nipped his earlobe and strummed one of his nipples with her index finger. Nothing he had ever known prepared him for the seductive power of her mouth sucking little eddies of heat over his jawline.

She was a delicate vibration against his skin. She was cozy warmth. She was the lovely scent of sex and beer and spice. She was the flutter of something new and fresh and expectant in the depths of his weary soul.

Oh, hell. He was in serious trouble here.

Even so, he couldn't stop himself from appreciating the feel of her soft body curled against his lap. Her hair glistened in the lamplight.

"You're the most beautiful thing I've ever seen," he whispered.

"I'm not beautiful," she denied. "My forehead is too wide."

"A sign of intelligence," he proclaimed, stunned that she did not recognize the power of her own beauty.

"My eyes are too squinchy."

"I adore your eyes. They're my favorite feature of yours."

"They are?" She smiled and those adorable little eyes in question almost disappeared into the folds of her eyelids. "You're such a liar. Men always go for my legs."

He angled a glance down at her legs. "I'm not denying you've got world-class legs, Princess, but it's those eyes that have me by the short hairs."

"Really?" She sounded incredulous.

"Really."

"My father says he doesn't know how I can see out of them, they're so small."

"I'm sorry, but your father sounds like a grade-A ass to me."

"He is," she admitted. "But he is my dad. I guess if my mother had lived everything would have been different, but she didn't and that's the way it is."

"Well, I do have to thank him for bringing you into this world."

"I was something of a disappointment. He wanted a boy."

"I have to say, I'm really glad you weren't a boy."

"I guess I've spent my entire life trying to make up for being female."

"I've spent my life trying to make up for having even been born." Beau shook his head. "My mother still blames me for her stretch marks."

"Family." Marissa chuckled. "Can't live with 'em, can't kill 'em."

The sexy ambience had dissipated in light of their conversation, but Beau was determined not to let the mood slip away.

"Where were we?" he murmured as he kissed Marissa's neck and stroked her smooth, flat belly. "The gallant knight had just introduced the sweet virgin to life's most carnal pleasures. You know we've got to put this into the video game."

"Absolutely." Her eyes went from his face, to his chest and then dropped down to his erection. "Oh-ho, what do we have here?"

"The better to love you with, my dear."

"That's the Big Bad Wolf. Different game."

"So it is. Shall we ride this great steed together?" He rocked the chair. "Do you feel my horse gallop?"

"I feel him all right." She giggled.

It struck him then that he'd never heard her giggle. She'd laughed a couple of times, but mostly that had been rueful laughter at her own expense. He'd never heard this lighthearted, free-spirited giggle before. The merry sound unfurled a soft, achy feeling deep inside his heart. He'd succeeded. He was teaching her how to have fun.

Leaning back in the rocker, he grasped her around the waist, raised her up and turned her in his lap so she was straddling him and her legs dangled off the sides of the chair. Slowly, he eased her down onto his flourishing shaft.

She hissed in her breath as he entered her in increments. She was still wet and warm from the hand job he'd given her.

"Ride me," he commanded and she began to rock, clinging to his neck like a horsewoman to a bridle. She threw back her head, exposing her throat, her hair brushing against her shoulders.

Perspiration purled over their conjoined bodies as they rocked. She arched her back and pressed her breast against his mouth, silently begging him to take the nipple between his teeth.

He complied and she uttered a strangled exclamation of supreme pleasure. He suckled that beaded nub, caressing it with his lips, his teeth, his tongue.

"No more of that," she gasped and broke from his mouth. "Too intense."

"Okay, try this." Grasping her hips, he guided her to a new rhythm—harder, faster, flying—while at the same time capturing her lips for a soul-searing kiss.

Leaning forward, bracing her knees against the slated spokes on the back of the chair, she raised and lowered herself while they rocked. It was a crazy sensation—at once up and down and back and forth.

She rubbed the tips of her breasts against his chest hairs and devoured his kisses. Her movements were strong and sure as she met his passion and raised the stakes even higher, thrusting her tongue deep in the warm recesses of his mouth.

Sensation built upon sensation, escalating swiftly in a blind, maddening rush. Reality slithered away and he felt as if he were piloting a rocket headed straight for the sun, soaring to a place where every molecule in his body threatened to dissolve into a timeless everything.

And then he cried her name as every vibrant, glowing cell inside him fragmented and shattered and when it was over, Beau felt more connected to Marissa than he ever had to anyone.

She was what he'd been searching for his entire life. A strong link, a solid tie, an unbreakable union with a cosmic something totally outside himself and yet wholly an integral part of his being.

At the sound of his cry, Marissa went rigid. She sank her teeth into his neck, not hurting him but holding her steady as he spilled his seed.

And he realized she had come, too.

The rocker slowed.

Their hearts slammed in unison, one meshed atop the other, beating as a single entity. She rested her forehead against his and they stared deeply into each other's eyes—falling, spinning, spiraling out into the bottomless depths of their souls.

The rocker stopped.

Finally, Marissa stirred above him and he became aware of the strain in his thighs, the cramp in his foot. He held tight to her waist. He didn't want her to get up. Didn't want this precious loving to ever end.

And that's when Beau knew he was doing it again, equating sex with love.

You've got to stop this, man. She has her life, you've got yours and in no way do they match. You have the next several weeks together. And that will be enough.

But no matter how hard he tried, Beau couldn't shake the feeling that no matter how long he lived, he could never get enough of Marissa.

FRANCINE PHILLIPS was right, Marissa marveled. Truly transcendental sex really did include a light-hearted sense of whimsy.

Wow.

She lay snuggled beside Beau in his bed, staring up at the ceiling and grinning like a fool, while he slept with one strong arm thrown over her waist.

All these years she'd seriously underestimated the power of play in the bedroom.

Fun. Games. Frivolity.

The words went up and down, around and around in her head like a merry-go-round.

Wow, wow, wow.

It was true. Orgasms were stronger, the fireworks hotter, the sex just plain better when you teased and flirted and relaxed. She'd thought she'd known what good sex was but she'd been wrong, wrong, wrong. How could she have been so blind?

Nothing had ever felt like this…this…

Wow.

Beau stirred beside her. "What are you grinning about?" he murmured, tickling her bare belly with his fingertips.

"How do you know I'm grinning?" she asked, the effervescent joy permeating her voice unmistakable. "It's dark in here."

"'Cause you keep making these little giggly sighs of pleasure. And because I've got the same damn grin on my face."

"I thought you were asleep."

"No, Princess, I was just lying low, getting my second wind."

"What game shall we play this time?"

"Ah," he said. "I see I have converted you."

"I was thinking maybe Truth or Dare," she said.

"Convert, hell, you've skipped right to expert," he growled and pulled her tight against his chest. "Have you ever played Truth or Dare?"

"No," she said. "But it sounds fun."

"Mostly," he said, "it's embarrassing."

"So which is it?" She chuckled as he licked her chin. "Truth or dare?"

"With the mood you're in, I'm sort of afraid to touch dare, so truth."

"Okay then. What is your sexiest fantasy?"

"I think we just acted it out."

"Nope, that's cheating. You have to tell the truth. The whole truth." A thrill raced through Marissa as she waited, breath bated for Beau to spill his most sensual daydream. "What is it? A threesome with you and two buxom babes?"

"I'm not saying that fantasy hasn't crossed my mind," he admitted. "I am a guy after all, but it's not my favorite fantasy."

"Let's hear it."

"You sure?"

"Just how kinky is this fantasy?"

"I never said it was kinky. We're talking hot here."

"I'm all ears." The pillow talk was generating some high-end sparks in the center of her solar plexus.

"Mirrors," he said.

"Mirrors?" Her voice rose.

"And candles."

"Go on."

"Mirrors on the ceiling, on the walls, on the floor. The room is a virtual cube of mirrors."

Marissa licked her lips as her mind conjured up the image.

"There's no bed, no furniture, just the smooth re-

flective glass and hundreds of candles burning all
across the floor.''

"Oh my.''

"The candles are scented. All sorts of flavors. Va-
nilla and cinnamon. Chocolate and coffee. Peaches
and honey.''

"Uh-huh.'' Her heart was strumming faster, the
pulse at her wrist beat quick and thready. Her
breathing was hot and shallow.

"My lover comes into the room. She's wearing a
mask.''

"Here comes the kinky part,'' Marissa teased.
"What else is she wearing?''

"Thong panties, pasties, thigh-high stockings and
stilettos.''

"Hey, you hypocrite.'' She tickled him under the
arm until he squirmed. "You had me believing you
hated high heels.''

"That's in real life. This is a fantasy.''

"Right. So continue.''

"I'm completely mesmerized by the sight of our
bodies moving together. Everywhere I look, up,
down, right, left, I see our reflections as we grope and
embrace and arouse each other.''

"Yeah, yeah,'' she egged him on.

"My lover gives me the most incredible floor show
of my life. She has me sit against the wall and then
she begins to dance. Pasties whirling, she slowly
strips off her panties and stockings. She dances with
her legs wide apart. If I look down at the mirrored
floor, I can see everything. Her most intimate parts

are exposed to me and she loves how horny she's making me.''

Marissa was panting now as her imagination spiraled into that mirrored fantasy room with Beau and she became the masked woman dancing for his pleasure.

''She asks me if I like the view. I tell her it's beautiful because it is. And then she starts stroking herself, showing me what feels good, demonstrating exactly what she wants me to do to her.''

His voice was low and throaty and filled with sex. Marissa's hand crept to his waist and slowly she walked her fingers down to his rock-hard erection. He groaned at her touch.

''Don't stop talking.''

She heard him gulp and then he continued. ''She gives me a lap dance, twisting lower and lower. The gates to her heaven are wide open, swollen with wanting me. And then she slips me inside her. We watch ourselves in the mirrors. Watch as I disappear in and out of her, gleaming and wet in the candlelight.''

''That's some fantasy you've got going on there. My turn now.''

''Truth or dare,'' he croaked, his voice sandpaper rough.

''Dare,'' she said.

''I knew you were going to pick that one.''

''Dare,'' she repeated.

''Okay.'' He breathed in a raspy sigh. ''I dare you to do it with me in front of the bathroom mirror.''

In unison, they tumbled from the bed and, laughing, sprinted straight for the bathroom. They skidded to a halt in front of the mirror and stared at their reflections.

Who was that silly-looking woman with the huge grin on her face?

"Just look at you," Beau said with admiration. "Baby, you've got it."

"You're not half-bad yourself." She winked.

They giggled and laughed and hummed. They stared at each other in the mirror as they caressed. Beau gently massaged Marissa's nipples between his thumbs and index fingers. She stroked Beau's thick, hard cock, dressing him in a condom.

They touched, toyed, gazed at their bodies with uninhibited glee. They kissed and fondled and licked and nibbled.

Then, at last, when neither of them could stand the toe-curling tension one more second, Beau gently turned and pressed Marissa toward the countertop. The smooth Formica was shockingly cool against her hot, damp breast. She hissed her breath in through her teeth.

"That's right, sweetheart. Sizzle for me."

Beau clamped both hands around her waist and rested his throbbing shaft against the feminine split of her cheeks. Gently, he spread her apart with his hand and made sure she was well lubricated.

"Do you want this?" he asked.

"Yes, yes. I want you. Now."

Gently, slowly, he entered her inch by inch. The torture was exquisite.

"I want all of you," she begged, thrashing her head and moaning low in her throat. "Now, now."

He plunged himself all the way in and she cried out. "Yes, oh yes."

His body covered hers. He filled her up.

Beau leaned forward, his stomach pressed against her back, his body moving in a slow, seductive rhythm, escalating the tension. With his right hand, he reached around her hips and lightly caressed the juncture between her thighs, all the while keeping up the steady pace of his strokes.

The sensation was blindingly dazzling. Marissa caught sight of their reflection in the mirror; Beau's face a twist of pure masculine ecstasy. The pressure intensified, building, building, building. She was so wet, so achy, so desperate to come again.

"Yes, yes. Don't stop, don't stop."

He moved wildly now, his control gone. He cried out low and hoarse, and while she watched, he came.

She followed with her own release seconds later and this frantic, thrashing climax was much more intense than the other two she'd already had that night.

A keening wail trailed from her throat as they tumbled together into that sweetest of all bliss.

Nothing had ever felt so good, so right.

Then Beau was kissing her with gentle kisses. On the back of the head, on the nape of her neck. Tenderly, he scooped her into his arms and carried her back to bed. She lay limp in his arms, totally spent, totally relaxed, with only one thought echoing in her head.

Where have you been all my life, Beau Thibbedeaux?

AFTER THEIR FIRST TIME together, they began working on the video game in earnest.

Their days were filled with scripting scenarios and coding the software. Their nights were spent acting out their wildest sexual fantasies.

They worked. They played. They made love. Again and again and again until they were sore and chapped and raw. And they savored every exquisite lovemaking-induced ache and pang.

They made love outdoors, in the back seat of Beau's car, in the boathouse. They acted out X-rated versions of *Beauty and the Beast*, *Phantom of the Opera* and "Little Red Riding Hood."

They took baths together and gave each other massages and shampooed each other's hair. They had sexy bedroom picnics, doing very naughty things with all manner of foods. They experimented with fabrics and feathers and blindfolds.

They played strip poker and strip Scrabble and strip chess. They danced. They sang. They laughed. They splashed in mud puddles and blew bubbles and rode scooters.

They banged on Beau's drum set and jumped on his pogo stick and walked on his stilts. They skipped stones over the river and tossed the Frisbee to Anna and sat on the back-porch rocking chairs for hours on end.

They went shopping and bought Marissa casual, carefree clothes. He talked her into buying cargo pants and tailored T-shirts that made her look impossibly cute. She wore the garments proudly with pink high-top sneakers. And to reward her for giving up her business clothes and stilettos, he gifted her with whimsical earrings.

But Marissa wasn't the only one who'd changed.

His "on hold" career was up and running again and he was happier than he'd been in a long time. With the new project came a new fire. Beau did two-dimensional mock-ups for the game on the computer and they reviewed them together every night. He was blown away by the creativity Marissa sparked in him. He confessed to her it was the best work he'd ever done and she was the reason.

He had the joy of watching her blossom under his tutelage. He coaxed and cajoled. He teased and flirted. He did everything in his power to help her relax and learn to enjoy herself.

She went from the hard-drive, uptight, competitive businesswoman to a giggly, laid-back hedonist who rarely wore shoes at all much less those killer high heels, and he could scarcely believe the alterations in her or that he'd been the one responsible for them. Although he realized once she was back in New York she would probably revert to her old ways.

Still, a part of him couldn't help hoping some measure of his influence would remain as his gift to her.

Because she had changed him as much as he'd changed her. He hadn't truly realized how much of a hermit he'd become until she'd drawn him out of himself.

Impossibly quick, five weeks slipped away and he was saddened to realize the project was almost ready for its debut run-through at the virtual-reality chamber in New Orleans. Their time together was rapidly drawing to a close.

When Beau realized Marissa had booked the virtual-reality chamber for the weekend before Mardi Gras, he decided to plot a grand seduction. With Remy's help, he called in a lot of old favors, spent way too much money and wrangled a balcony suite on Bourbon Street for the four days. Four days partying with Marissa in the Big Easy. If it were four hundred days, it would never be enough.

Because no matter how hard he tried to deny it, no matter how hard he kept telling himself their relationship was just about sex, in his heart he knew it wasn't true.

13

"I'M REALLY GOING to miss you." Jenny sighed, folding one of Marissa's sweaters and passing it over for her to pack into her suitcase. "It's been fun having another woman my age around."

"I'm going to miss you, too." Marissa tucked the sweater on top of the pin-striped suit she hadn't put on since the day Beau had insisted she wear casual clothes. "We'll still keep in touch. E-mail. Telephone. You can even come visit me in New York when you take a vacation."

"It's not the same." Jenny shook her head ruefully. "And I run the B and B. There's no such thing as a vacation."

"So then I'll come back to see you."

"Will you? Really?"

"Of course."

"It wouldn't be weird for you? Seeing Beau again."

"Weird?" Marissa pretended she didn't know what Jenny was talking about. In truth, she was struggling hard to deny the feelings Beau stirred inside her. Mushy, hopeful feelings she had no business feeling. "Why would it be weird?"

"I dunno. It's usually kind of embarrassing when you run into an old fling."

"Jenny," she said. "Beau and I are cool."

"Honestly?" Jenny sounded hopeful.

"Honestly. We both got what we wanted. We had a good time. No hard feelings on either side."

"I hope you're right. I love you both and would hate to see either one of you hurt."

Marissa cocked her head and angled Jenny a pensive glance. "Has Beau said anything to you to indicate his feelings for me are anything more than casual?"

Her heart thumped. She wanted Jenny to say no, but something deep inside her ached for her to say yes.

The paradoxical emotions startled her. She wasn't a romantic. She didn't need undying declarations of love. Her affair with Beau had been exactly what she wanted. He'd helped her so much. He'd taught her how to have fun in bed and she would be forever grateful. But that's all there was to it.

Gratitude.

"Noooo," Jenny said. "He's never said anything."

"There you go." Marissa held out both palms. "Nothing to worry about. He's fine. I'm fine."

"It's just that he seems…"

"What?" She hung there, waiting for Jenny's words, not knowing why she felt so nervous.

"I think maybe he's…" Jenny stopped, shrugged. "I'm probably imagining things."

Part of Marissa wanted to press Jenny to explain

her intuitive feelings, but part of her was terrified to hear the answer, so she said nothing. Instead, she embraced Jenny in a warm hug.

She had never been close to another woman. As a military brat it had been difficult for her to forge deep attachments. She'd learned to accept relationships as temporary, and until coming to Louisiana the transient nature of her friendships had never bothered her. Yet something about this place, these people, had really gotten under her skin and she realized how much she was truly going to miss everyone.

But Marissa belonged in New York and she knew it. This small respite from the city had been good for her, but she couldn't wait to get home. Couldn't wait to accept the directorship and move into her new office.

Her old competitive feelings came rushing to the forefront of her mind, pushing out these new softer, reflective emotions. Yes, rather than spend time dwelling on what she was leaving behind, she would focus on what lay ahead.

The future beckoned. Her promotion, more money, the success she'd been seeking. When she imagined telling her father the good news, her spirits soared and she started thinking about the new pair of shoes she would buy to replace the lost Jimmy Choos.

But in spite of her bravado, despite her assertion that she was happy and eager to return home, a sad wistful lump weighted her stomach.

She was seriously going to miss Beau. She thought of his endearing smile, his slow way of walking, how his touch set her skin on fire. She felt an inexplicable urge to cry, but she wasn't a crybaby. She was tough and sensible. She was General Dwight D. Sturgess's daughter. She could handle anything.

Besides, she and Beau had four more days together. Four more days to live it up in New Orleans. Four more days to make lasting memories. Four more days to enjoy the game.

She could do it. And then she would simply let him go. She was very good at goodbyes.

No matter how her heart ached she knew it was the only pragmatic thing to do.

MARISSA AND BEAU stood inside the newly constructed virtual-reality chamber dubbed the Cavern on the grounds of Tulane University. Marissa had on her olive-green cargo pants, a red T-shirt, pink high-top sneakers, and her ears sported the sweet earrings Beau had bought for her.

The Cavern measured twelve-by-twelve-by-ten feet and featured three twelve-foot screens. They wore 3-D goggles and held special pressure-sensitive joystick wands. They had a broadband connection to the Pegasus programmers in New York while local technicians and students manned the regional computers.

Marissa took a deep breath, realizing they were going to be living out virtual-reality sex scenes right in front of the technicians. It was all part of the job. She could do it and live through it. Thank heavens, the human images were computer animations and not actual physical replicas of her and Beau.

"Ready to rock and roll?" the supervising technician called out from the control booth.

Beau gave a thumbs-up sign and nodded.

The technician flipped a switch and the screens came to life. Marissa's breath hitched as she recognized the scene.

The hero, casually dressed and grinning, lounged in a rocking chair on a mock-up of Greenbrier's front porch. The heroine, dressed in a business suit, a tight grimace on her face, marched up the steps on killer stilettos.

Marissa swallowed hard.

"I'm going to teach you to have fun," the hero said, slowly rising to his feet. "Together we're going to learn what good sex is really all about."

Marissa poked her tongue against the inside of her cheek. Something about the hero's high-handed ways irritated her. Even though she'd written the dialogue herself, she hadn't realized until now how arrogant it made him sound. She made a mental note to revise the script.

The hero took the heroine's hand and they walked into the plantation. Then, the scene shifted to find the hero dressed as the knight and the heroine in a white sheath. The knight came across the room toward her.

The hairs on Marissa's arms lifted at the echo of his boots against the wooden floor. The scent of leather and spicy cologne wafted toward her nose through tiny tubes in the headset. She turned her head to the left and saw a four-poster bed in the corner. Panning to the right she peered out a window and in the distance spied the king's men riding up on horses. The scene that had blossomed in her imagination the night she and Beau first made love was now utterly real and splashed on three giant screens surrounding them.

She was embarrassed and proud all at the same time and her conflicting emotions confused her.

When the knight reached out and caressed the heroine's shoulder, it felt as if her own shoulder was being caressed. She stepped back and the computer tracked her movements and adjusted the view. Now the knight was slowly unbuttoning his shirt. Marissa shivered at the vividness of the experience.

Talk about déjà vu.

Unnerved, she waved her wand and the scenery shifted. The knight and the virgin disappeared and she found herself in another segment of the game.

This room featured a jungle scene complete with a waterfall and leopards. Beau followed her. This time, he was dressed in a loincloth and she was his female companion. The air smelled ripe with the humid perfume of rich tropical flowers and exotic fruits.

Like kids playing tag, they went from scene to scene, room to room, exploring the world they had created both in real life and for the game. For an hour, they played. And when they reached the end, Marissa felt edgy and breathless but even if pressed she couldn't say why.

Right before her eyes, she watched the heroine change. The female character grew looser, laxer, and she began imitating the hero. She was having fun, yes, but her whole personality was disappearing. She wasn't the aggressive, smartly dressed business-woman who'd marched up the plantation steps in the beginning of the game.

She'd lost her drive and her ambitions along with her inhibitions.

But it was good. Right? That was the point. To change. To learn to relax and have fun and truly enjoy her sexuality.

Why then did she feel as if she'd lost something important? Why were her knees quaking? Why was her stomach in knots? Why did she have the urge to run to the control booth, rip the software from the computers and destroy it?

Marissa watched as the hero gently cupped the heroine's cheek and she felt the soft caress of *Beau's* fingers on *her* skin.

The animated hero kissed the animated heroine but it was Beau's lips brushing Marissa's, Beau's scent filling her nostrils, Beau's taste exploding in her mouth.

She was totally, utterly blown away at the very same time she was appalled. His creative genius exceeded anything she could have imagined, and yet his will had quietly, insidiously taken her over.

Marissa was about to remove her goggles but realized there was another scene. Beau had added a postscript to the ending without telling her.

Her body tensed.

''Now,'' the hero murmured to the heroine. ''You

have changed for the better. You've learned not to take yourself or life quite so seriously.''

What! What!

Something about the animated hero's delivery of his speech sent a spear of anger arrowing through her body. His pronouncement was egotistical, as if he held all the secrets to the heroine's sexual awakening. As if he was solely in control and she was his puppet.

Is that how Beau saw their relationship? Did he believe he was doing her this big huge favor by showing her how to have fun?

What in the hell are you talking about, Marissa? These are pretend people. This is an imaginary game.

Based on reality.

The reality of the past six weeks spent making love with Beau.

And there it was on the screen for everyone to see. How he'd changed her. Manipulated her. Her chest squeezed and she found it hard to breathe.

Oh God, she was losing it. Her head spun with the realization she'd been tricked. By Beau, by Baxter and Jackson, by Judd, by Dash, by her own emotions.

Claustrophobia enveloped her. She had to get out of here. She had to think. She had to breathe.

With a trembling hand, she ripped off the goggles and ran from the chamber.

"Marissa?'' Beau followed her out of the virtual-reality chamber and into the corridor. He found her getting a drink from the water fountain. "Are you all right?''

Marissa straightened and turned to face him. He saw her hand trembling and knew at once that something in the game had disturbed her.

He wanted to reach for her but something in her rigid body language warned him off. "What's wrong?"

She turned and he took in the straight, prim slash of her mouth, the coolness clouding her dark brown eyes, the closing off of her energy. He felt as if he was standing before a stone-cold fireplace on a winter's day in Montana.

"Talk to me. Tell me what's wrong."

She clenched her jaw and shook her head.

"Obviously, I've upset you somehow, but how can I fix it if you won't discuss the issue with me?"

"I'm feeling too angry to speak to you right now."

"It's okay to be angry. Just talk to me."

"All right, but remember you asked for this."

"Lay it on the line."

"Here's the message I got from the game. You think you're better than me," she accused. "That your way of life is superior to mine."

"Whoa!" He raised his palms. "Where is this coming from?"

"From your arrogance," she hissed.

He was completely taken aback. He certainly hadn't expected this response from her when he'd hurriedly coded the ending of the game. What he'd intended was to show her how much he admired her for having the courage to change. Couldn't she see that? How had he bungled things? He'd meant to honor her, not distress her.

"What are you talking about?" He frowned in confusion. "I don't understand."

"Are you really so high and mighty you don't see what's right under your nose?"

"See what?" God, she was driving him crazy. He pushed a hand through his hair.

"You've manipulated me into becoming *your* ideal woman. You've altered me until I don't even recognize myself." She swept her hand at her outfit. "Cargos, a T-shirt, sneakers. I've never worn anything like this in my entire life."

"But you picked the outfit."

"I chose the damn things to please you. Because I thought you wanted me to wear stuff like this." She smacked her forehead with her palm. "I'm such a fool. I bent over backward to please you the same way I've always turned myself into a pretzel to please my father. With him, I do it by pushing myself to succeed. With you, I did it by playing your games."

"Calm down. You're overreacting."

"Am I? You can't deny it, Beau. It's right there in your script. You're patting yourself on the back for adapting me like you adapted one of your games. Well, I'm not a marionette and I refuse to let you pull the strings." She jerked his silly earrings off her ears and flung them on the ground.

"Hey, now, wait just a minute. You were the one who asked me to help you learn to how to have fun," he challenged.

"And you took advantage of that request."

"I know what's happening here. You're taking the anger you've always felt toward your father, but were too afraid to express, and you're projecting it onto me. Well bring it on, sweetheart." He made "gimme" motions with his fingers. "I can take anything you can dish out."

"Oh, that cheap pop psychology is so lame." She placed her hands on her hips and glared at him. "And completely untrue."

"Is it?" He hardened his jaw and narrowed his eyes.

"Totally."

"Then why are you so upset with me?"

"Because you've turned me into this…this… this…" she sputtered.

"This what?"

"This submissive accommodating woman." She flung her arms in the air.

"From my point of view, you're not looking very submissive or accommodating at this moment."

"That's because seeing the video game wised me up to what's been going on."

He shook his head. "Listen to yourself. You're the one who came to me. I was perfectly happy until you showed up."

"Yeah. Happy hanging out in bars and doing nothing with your life."

"What's this really all about? Why are you lashing out? What have I done that's so horrible?"

"You've turned me into something I'm not," she cried.

"What are you, Marissa? Do you even know? Maybe there's where the problem lies. *You* don't really know who you are."

She stared at him and in that instant she looked like a lost kid. She seemed so fragile right now that to touch her would be to break her.

"You've misunderstood me," he said softly, feeling as if he was trying to talk a jumper down from a ledge. She was spooked. Big-time. "I never intended to change you or make you feel manipulated. I'm sorry if I've done anything that's caused you to doubt yourself."

"Don't try to placate me." Her nostrils flared delicately.

"I'm not."

"Jenny told me about your relationship with your mother. How you curried favors to get on her good side. I'm not falling for it."

"Falling for what, sweetheart?"

"Your apology."

It wasn't easy to woo a woman with a steely look in her eyes and a gigantic chip on her shoulder. Beau didn't know how to reach her, but he ached at her pain. The closer Marissa skated to the edge, the calmer he became.

"I realize the video game has triggered some deep-seated fear in you. A virtual-reality game can sometimes be too real and our game is definitely art reflecting life. We lived that game, you and I."

"Yes, we did."

"You've changed a lot in a short period of time and you're afraid that when you get back to New York, the new Marissa might not fit in so well anymore."

She said nothing and Beau hoped he was getting through to her. He lowered his voice. "Besides, you left too soon. You didn't get to watch all of the game. In the last segment, the hero proves to the heroine he loves her for who she is. Even when she's angry at him. Even when they don't agree. They still have a bond. They're still connected. No silly spat, no heated argument affects the way he feels about her."

"Really?" She swallowed hard. He could see that she wanted to believe in him, that she longed to trust in what he was saying.

"I don't blame you for being uncertain," he soothed and moved toward her. He was grateful when she didn't step away. "Your whole worldview is changing. A lot of your long-held values are crumbling. That's pretty scary stuff. Learning that you can let go of years of mistaken beliefs. But I'm here, Marissa, you're not going to chase me away."

"Why not?" she asked, unshed tears gleaming in her eyes.

"Don't you realize how truly extraordinary you are? Whether you're competing or relaxing, having fun or working hard. Hollering at me or making love to me. I accept you. No rules. No strings. With me you don't need to be anything more than you already are."

She bit down on her thumbnail.

He held out his hand to her, his heart thumping crazy with the fear she would turn away.

And then wonderfully, miraculously, she smiled tentatively and reached out to him.

14

BEAU HAD BEEN RIGHT, Marissa conceded. She had overreacted because she was afraid. She was scared to death she was falling in love with him and she didn't know how to deal with her feelings.

And when she was afraid, she had a tendency to lash out. Seeking to protect herself through aggression.

The amazing thing was, he hadn't let her anger or her intensity chase him off. He'd stayed and calmly insisted she face her fears.

Because of his refusal to allow her to get away with hiding her feelings behind a tough offense, she'd had the most magnificent weekend of her life and she was grateful to him.

It was Tuesday afternoon and Mardi Gras was in full swing. Marissa sat on the second-floor balcony of their hotel. She took a sip of champagne and gazed out at the river of people rippling and undulating below.

She'd couriered the video game to Judd the day before, and he had just called to praise the quality of the software and congratulate her on her new job. She was dressed in a business suit and her remaining stilettos—Judd's call had interrupted a rousing game of success-oriented businesswoman and her accommodating male secretary.

Music, laughter and rowdy voices mingled, producing a cacophony of sound. Women on balconies across and around them lifted their shirts to the crowd, flashing their assets and receiving cheap strands of beads in return for the show. A hundred different aromas drifted on the air—crawfish, beer, cayenne pepper, hot dogs combined with the pungent spice of ten thousand human bodies crushed together on one narrow street.

Judd's call hadn't brought all happy news, however. He wanted her there with him when he presented the game to Francine Phillips on Thursday morning. That meant Marissa would have to leave New Orleans tomorrow afternoon at the latest.

She didn't want to go.

"Why are you frowning?" Beau asked. He came over and pressed the tips of two fingers between her eyebrows. Marissa looked up at him and her heart lurched.

"I'm having fun," she said.

"Funny way to show it. Frowning so fierce."

"I was just thinking hard."

"Uh-oh, sounds serious," he teased and plunked down beside her in the adjoining rocking chair. "What are you thinking so hard about?"

"You. Me. Us."

"Us?" Was it her imagination, or did he sound hopeful?

"We've had a great time together."

"Yes, we have."

"A few misunderstandings."

"All relationships have a few bumps." He smiled.

"I want to apologize for getting wonky on you in the virtual-reality chamber."

He waved a hand. "It's forgotten."

"You were right. I got scared. The game brought out all my insecurities."

It wasn't the best of times for an intimate conversation, not while the party to end all parties raged around them, but Marissa felt compelled to tell him what she was thinking before she lost her courage.

Blame it on the champagne, the crazy "anything goes" atmosphere, and the fact that time was slipping away from them, or maybe even all three excuses rolled into one. Something loosened her tongue. Her words came out in a rush as if desperate to escape before she slapped them in lockdown.

"You want to know something?" he asked, taking her hand and gently circling her palm with his thumb.

"What?"

"The video game shook me up, too."

"Oh?"

"There we were on-screen. Our sexual adventures on display for everyone to see."

She nodded. The warmth of his thumb sent little eddies of pleasure spiraling up her arm and clouding her thought process. Closing her eyes, she leaned into the pleasure. She was going to miss this. More than she would ever have guessed.

Emotion clogged her throat. No more talking. It was time for action.

She got to her feet, took Beau's hand and led him into the bedroom. He closed the balcony door behind them, shutting out the noise, closing out the world, leaving room for only the two of them.

Grinning, Marissa bounced onto the middle of the bed and lifted her top, flashing him to show she wasn't wearing a bra.

He growled low in his throat and stalked toward her.

Quickly, she lowered her top. ''Uh-uh. Where're my beads?''

''Sorry, all out.'' He shook his head.

''No beads, no play.''

''Would you settle for a pearl necklace?'' Chuckling, he settled his knees on the edge of the bed and reached for her.

''You're outrageous.''

''And you love it.''

''Come here, buccaneer.'' She grabbed his shoulders and pulled him toward her.

''So we're playing booty pirate and island castaway again?''

''You know me so well,'' she murmured but got no further as his lips stole hers and he pushed her back against the pillows.

They made short work of their clothes, slinging tops and bottoms and undies willy-nilly around the room.

''This time,'' Marissa said. ''I'm a lady booty pirate and you're a shipwrecked computer geek who has invaded my Caribbean lair.''

''Hmm. I like this one. Although I resent the fact I have to be a computer geek.''

''Silence!'' she commanded and pressed her palm firmly against his mouth. ''I've taken you captive and tied you to my bed.''

They switched places. Beau flat on his back, arms over his head, Marissa straddling his knees. She reveled in her position of power.

She sent him her most wicked grin then slowly lowered her mouth to his erection. Oh yum. He tasted so good. An instant rush of excitement spread through her body as he hardened and swelled inside her mouth.

Brushing his luscious protuberance with her tongue, she thrilled when he groaned and clutched her hair in his fists.

''Hands off. You're tied up, remember.''

Reluctantly, he let go of her head.

She swirled her tongue around the rim of him, until he was completely steamed up, his back arched, his body tense, waiting for the impending eruption.

And then she stopped.

''Vixen,'' he accused.

''You don't know the half of it, my computer geek,'' she said as she climbed on top of him and slowly, inch by lascivious inch, dropped her hips, encompassing him with her other lips. All the while, enjoying the dual expression of pleasure and torture flitting across his face.

She increased the tempo, letting him get the full experience of her fanny slapping against him, her eyes never leaving his face as she gauged his closeness to climax. She wasn't going to let him go over the edge. Not yet.

When he once more hovered on the brink, she pulled off him.

His groan was deeper, hungrier this time. "Witch."

"Insults will only earn you more punishment."

"Malicious wench, wicked harpy, naughty siren, sinful seductress."

"Oooh, you asked for it."

She gobbled him up. Nibbling, sucking, licking, nipping. She stroked and caressed and tasted.

"I can't stand it," he cried. "I'm about to blow my top."

She removed her mouth and climbed aboard his body again. Back and forth she switched. From the wet recesses of her mouth to the soft darkness of her most feminine cave.

"Please, Marissa," he begged. "Let me have it."

"Come on, big boy," she said. "Give me all you've got." Then she wrapped her mouth around him one more time and took him to the stars.

She gloried as he shattered into her and she partook of his delicious masculine essence. He trembled and shook. Marissa wrapped him in her arms and rested his head against her shoulder.

"Now," he said, several minutes later, after he'd recovered. "It's my turn to be the booty pirate."

He'd just gotten started, when a knock at the door

interrupted their game. They lay side by side, breathing hard and trying not to giggle.

"Do you suppose it's housekeeping?" Marissa asked.

"Shh," Beau whispered. "Maybe they'll go away."

The knock sounded again.

"We don't need any towels," Beau called out.

"It's not housekeeping," Remy answered.

In unison, they scrambled from the bed, searching desperately for their clothes strewn about the room.

"Just a minute, bro."

From the other side of the door, Remy's laugh was deep and hearty.

When they were dressed, Marissa perched in a chair by the desk while Beau opened the door. "What's up?"

Remy stepped into the room. "I hate to interrupt your private time. But I'm desperate and I've got nowhere else to turn."

"Problem?" Beau asked.

"Clint called in sick and I'm overwhelmed with the Mardi Gras crowd. Jenny's baby-sitting Sarah and Willis so Allie can help out at the bar but it's still more than we can handle. Beau, can you pitch in?"

"You don't even have to ask. I'm there."

Remy slapped his brother on the back. "Thanks, man. I better get going. Allie's by herself."

"I'm right behind you," Beau said.

Remy left and Beau turned to Marissa. "I hope you

can forgive me. I had a wonderful surprise planned for this evening, but Remy…''

"Don't worry about it.'' Marissa smiled and forced herself not to feel disappointed. How could she resent his devotion to his family? It was one of his most endearing qualities and she admired his loyalty more than she could say.

"But it's our last night together,'' he protested. ''This isn't fair to you.''

"Your brother needs your help. Go.''

"You're not upset?''

"I can't say I'm not feeling let down, but just because you have to work doesn't mean we can't spend the night together.'' She got up from the chair and looked around for her shoes. ''I'll come, too. Sounds like Remy can use all the hands he can get.''

"Really?'' Beau looked at her with admiration. ''You'd do that for me?''

"Sure. I want to be with you.'' It was true. She would do anything to spend the remainder of her time in New Orleans with Beau. ''Your brother needs help and I'll go home with wild stories of tending bar on Bourbon Street during Mardi Gras.''

"You ever tend bar?''

"No, but how hard could it be?''

"During Mardi Gras? Damn hard.''

"Are you forgetting who you're talking to, Mr. Thibbedeaux? I love a challenge.''

Beau gathered her in his arms, kissed her long and deep and then said, ''Princess, you're the greatest.''

SERVING DRINKS to the disorderly Mardi Gras crowd was much harder than it looked, Marissa quickly learned. As she poured beers into mugs or blended cocktails or measured out shots, the drunks mobbing the bar grew louder and rowdier and more suggestive with each passing hour. Twice she'd had her fanny pinched and once she'd had to slap a frat boy's hand for grabbing her breast.

Remy's bar was a total madhouse, packed wall to wall with carousing bodies. Blues music blared from the quartet onstage and several female patrons kept flashing their boobs for beads.

Every inch of her smelled of alcohol and she had cut her thumb slicing limes. She was hot and sweaty and her feet ached. She'd broken three glasses, burned a batch of popcorn and four times she'd gotten swindled by customers who walked off without paying their bar tab. But in spite of it all, Marissa was happy to be with Beau.

Beau and Remy and Allie worked beside her, mixing drinks, making change, wiping down the bar that quickly got wet and sticky again. They emptied ashtrays and refilled peanut bowls and repeatedly had to ask customers to climb down off the tables.

The night was humid. Overhead, the ceiling fans whirled but moved little air. Marissa's shirt stuck to her back. Beau reached around her to fish ice from the bin and his elbow grazed her waist.

''You looked exhausted,'' he said, his voice full of tenderness. ''Why don't you go on back to the hotel. We can manage.''

"What? And miss midnight on Bourbon Street during Mardi Gras?" She flashed him a grin.

"It's not as romantic as it sounds."

No, she thought. But being here with you is.

Beau moved away and Marissa took a deep breath. Okay, she had to stop thinking like this. The directorship in New York beckoned.

The problem was she wasn't so sure she wanted it anymore.

That alien thought seized her and she felt at once panicky and relieved. What had once been her be-all and end-all paled sharply in contrast to the life she'd been living for the past six weeks.

A life full of fun, adventure, sex, thrills and more. So very much more.

But who was she now if she wasn't the well-heeled businesswoman who'd marched into this very bar at the first of the year with the headstrong intention of recruiting Beau Thibbedeaux.

Who indeed?

What if you stayed? whispered the voice in the back of her brain. What would happen then?

The idea was so foreign, she had trouble imagining it.

And then she looked over at Beau and her heart just melted. He winked and gave her a lazy smile and in that moment, she knew.

She was in love with him.

Startled, she almost dropped the mug of beer she was pouring for a sassy drag queen.

The drag queen fixed a gaze on Beau and licked

his lips. "My, my, my, he's delicious. Do you know if he's straight or not?"

Jealousy shot through her. "Back off, Priscilla. He's mine."

"Meooow." The drag queen made clawing gestures at her with her fake crimson fingernails.

"Here's your beer, now take a hike."

"Relax, honey, I'm not gonna arm wrestle you for him. Competitive as you, you'd break my poor little wrist." In a swish of sequins and feathers, the drag queen sauntered off.

Good grief. Had she actually let the drag queen get to her? Marissa's heart was fluttering wildly and her face was flushed hot from the heady realization she was in love with Beau.

"Well, well, well, I see you haven't lost your edge in spite of your kinky affair with the software genius. Although I must admit, I never expected to find you behind a bar slinging booze."

Marissa jerked her head around to see Dash Peterson squeezing up to the bar, his sleazy grin firmly in place.

"What are you doing here?" she demanded.

"Slumming apparently." He waved a hand at the boisterous crowd.

"Why are you in New Orleans?"

He shrugged. "I came for Mardi Gras."

"Liar. I don't know what it is, but you're working some kind of angle. Well, you can forget about it. The directorship is mine, Peterson. Deal with it."

"Why, Marissa, you sound downright paranoid."

"What do you want?"

"I'll have a Manhattan," he said, his voice low and suggestive.

Ignoring his seductive tone, Marissa called out his drink order to Remy and glanced around to look for Beau, but he was nowhere in sight.

"No, I mean what do you want from me?" She narrowed her eyes at him. What was the slime bucket up to?

"Why, to collect on our bet."

"Huh?"

"Are you trying to tell me you've forgotten about our friendly little wager?"

"Oh, that." She shook her head. Over the course of the past six weeks she'd had so much fun with Beau she'd forgotten all about Dash and his silly, competitive wager. Indeed, it seemed aeons had passed since they'd glared each other down in the hallway of the Pegasus offices.

"You owe me a grand." He held out his palm. "Pay up."

"I'm not giving you a penny."

Dash rolled his eyes. "Oh, please, don't try to tell me you didn't sleep with him. I saw the video game. There's no way you two created something that provocative without steaming up the sheets together."

"My sex life is none of your business."

"I beg to differ. I have a thousand bucks riding on the outcome. Look me in the eye and tell me to my face you didn't bed him."

She didn't look at him.

''I knew it!'' Dash hooted. ''Kudos for having the balls to go all the way for your career. I'm proud of you. Luring the reluctant prospect into the sack with your sexual wiles is exactly like something the Dashmeister would do.''

Marissa felt sick to her stomach and she had a sudden desperate urge to take a shower. Viewed from the outside, it probably did look as if she'd bedded Beau simply to persuade him to sign the contract.

In the beginning, it was exactly like that, Marissa. Shame suffused her body.

Dash leaned closer. ''Face facts, Sturgess. You and I are two peas in a pod. We belong together.''

Marissa shuddered. ''I'm nothing like you.''

''Really? Are you so sure? I'm cutthroat and willing to do whatever it takes to win. Who else does that sound like?''

Oh God, he was right. She was like him.

''Manhattan's up.'' Remy set the drink at her elbow and hurried off to fill another order.

She snatched the glass and shoved it at Dash. ''Get out of here, now,'' she hissed.

''Not without my money.''

''We'll discuss this later, just go.''

''Give me a kiss first.''

''I won't.''

''You want me to tell your lover he was nothing more than a side bet?''

''You dirty rotten...'' she was about to say ''bastard'' but she didn't get the chance. Dash leaned over the bar and planted a kiss on her lips at the exact moment she heard the loud thwap of a case of beer being dropped on the floor behind her.

Whirling on her heels, she came face-to-face with Beau, her lips wet from Dash's sloppy kiss.

His gray eyes were smoky dark and unbearably cold and the look he gave her chilled Marissa to the bone.

Dear Lord, how much of their horrid conversation had he overheard?

HEART STAGGERING into his sternum, knees quaking, he turned, grabbed a bottle of whiskey from the bar and stalked out the back entrance.

"Beau!" Marissa cried from behind him. "I can explain everything."

His hands shook with fury as he twisted the cap off the whiskey bottle. Tossing back his head, he threw a hot, rough slug of harsh liquid down his throat. His head reeled, not from the potent alcohol but from the painful knowledge Marissa had played him for a chump.

He'd known all along she was competitive. That she would do whatever it took to get what she wanted. He shouldn't be surprised or hurt, but dammit he was. He'd never suspected she was so manipulative she would bet her colleague she could get him to design the video game by bedding him. She'd used him as a rung up her career ladder, stepping all over his heart in those cruel stilettos. He'd never meant anything to her.

And to think he'd been spinning what-if dreams

about their future. That he'd been planning on asking her to stay in Louisiana.

What an idiot he'd been.

He pushed through the back door of the bar. It slammed hard against the concrete wall and he marched into the alley. He took another slug of whiskey, gritting his teeth against the acrid rush.

"Beau." She followed him into the dimly lit alley. "Please wait."

The air was miserably humid, but cool. The raucous sounds of Mardi Gras echoed all around them from the bluesy wail of saxophones to steady drumbeats to drunken shrieks of laughter. But his mind hardly registered any of it.

"Stop walking and talk to me."

He whirled around, glaring hard and long. She winced and shrank back under the strength of his anger. "You really don't want to hear what I have to say right now. I advise you to go back inside."

"Let me have it." She hardened her chin. "Go on. I deserve it."

Instead, he took another swallow of alcohol and glared even harder.

"Booze isn't the answer," she said quietly.

"Mind your own business."

"Beau, please, you've got to let me explain the situation."

"I've sized the situation up accurately enough. You won the directorship you coveted over your pal in there by luring me into your bed. When you celebrate on a new pair of shoes this time, may I suggest something with a steel spike embedded in the heel, so you can just go ahead and stab the next guy right in the heart with it.''

''I'm so sorry, Beau.'' Her bottom lip trembled and she looked as if she was about to cry.

While the sight of his tough Marissa on the verge of tears wrenched at his gut, Beau stubbornly hardened his resolve against her.

''Will you forgive me?''

''You've put me through the wringer, Marissa. Squeezed me dry. I don't have anything left to give you.''

''It was never like that. I never planned to sleep with you. I never planned to fall—'' She broke off.

''What?'' He narrowed his eyes even more but his gut clenched. Was she about to confess that she'd fallen for him the way he'd fallen for her? But even if she did, would he believe her?

She reached out a hand to him but he pulled away. Sorrow twisted her features and she looked sadly older and wiser.

''Admit the truth,'' he said. ''You don't care about me. I'm just another notch on your belt. Another competition won.''

Fire flamed in her brown eyes. ''Okay, fine. Pout if you want. Act like a spoiled rich kid. I'm through begging for your forgiveness. I made a mistake. I'm not proud of myself, but I refuse to grovel. Especially to a man who insists I face the truth about my actions but continues to delude himself about his own.''

''Delude myself? What in the hell are you talking about?''

''You think you're so noble because you walked away from your job, from New York, from the people who were counting on you. You fled to Louisiana to hide out. You convinced yourself you did it to slow down, find peace, reconnect with your past, but the truth is, Beau, you did it for control. In your own weird way, you're as competitive as I am.''

''That's the stupidest thing I ever heard.'' Even as he denied what she was saying, a nagging suspicion she was correct gnawed at the back of his brain.

''Is it?''

''I don't need this crap.'' He turned from her before he said something he would forever regret.

''That's right,'' she hollered after him as he stalked off. ''Go ahead. Do what you do best. Quit. Give up the fight in order to preserve your fragile view of yourself. That's it. Run away.''

15

"CONGRATULATIONS, Marissa. This incredible virtual-reality game captures everything we wanted. Mind-blowing orgasms, Fourth of July fireworks and most of all a fun, lighthearted sense of whimsy. You and Mr. Thibbedeaux have far exceeded Baxter and Jackson's expectations," Francine Phillips enthused. "We're very pleased."

The Pegasus software team seated around the conference table broke into applause. All except for Dash, who shot Marissa a sour-grapes frown. She didn't have the spirit to shoot back an in-your-face-Peterson smirk.

"Thank you," Marissa said quietly.

It had been two weeks since she'd returned from New Orleans. Two miserable weeks where she'd been unable to think of anything except Beau and the awful way she'd hurt him.

She'd gotten what she wanted. She was the new account director. She had an office with a partial view of Central Park. She'd even received several calls from headhunters looking to recruit her for some of the top software design firms in the country. But the victory felt completely hollow. Her success had cost her Beau's respect and the price had been way too high.

"So pleased, in fact," Francine continued, "we want to commission a sequel to the game."

She should have been elated by Francine's words. She should have been slapping high fives with the programmers and doing a little hip-bumping dance with Judd. She should have been picking out her next pair of outrageously overpriced shoes.

Instead, she felt depressed. "I'm not sure Mr. Thibbedeaux would be willing to reprise his role as designer."

"You convinced him the first time, you can do it again," Francine said. "We have faith in you."

Marissa felt the heat of Judd's gaze on her face. In a moment of weakness, she'd broken down and told him what had happened between she and Beau.

"I've never seen you so twisted up over a man," Judd had said. "Are you sure you're not in love with him?"

But that was the thing. She was in love with him. Stone cold in love and there was nothing to be done about it.

Judd cleared his throat. "Francine, Marissa is awfully busy with her new position, I think we're going to have to turn down the assignment."

"Wh-what?" Francine sputtered. "Oh, wait, I get it. This is about more money, isn't it. All right then, I've been authorized to increase the price by ten percent. Will that be enough to entice Marissa to return to Louisiana?"

"It's not about the money," Judd said. "We're going to pass on creating a second game."

Marissa lifted her head to stare at her boss. Had she heard him right? He held her gaze.

"Sometimes, you have to get your priorities straight."

What was he saying? That he was going to turn down this huge offer because of her. Marissa splayed a palm over her chest and shook her head. "Don't refuse on my behalf, Judd."

"I don't want to lose you, Marissa. You're the best account manager I ever had."

"Hey!" Dash protested but everyone ignored him.

"We'll take the project, Francine, but only if you agree to a different designer. Thibbedeaux really is retired for good," Judd said.

"But we want Thibbedeaux."

"Then you'll have to go and get him yourself." Marissa got to her feet. She couldn't stay here a minute longer. Not with Judd being so kind and backing her up one hundred percent. Not when her heart was aching to be in Louisiana. She had to get out of the room before she dissolved into a fountain of girlie tears. "If you'll excuse me."

She left the conference room, biting down hard on the inside of her cheek to keep from crying, and rushed into her office. She shut the door behind her, plunked down into her chair and dropped her face into her hands.

How long was this going to hurt? She'd never pined over a man. Never longed for a place the way she longed for Fleur de Luna, Louisiana. Never yearned to be part of a couple, a community.

But now she was making up for lost time, pining and longing and yearning with a fierceness that took her breath.

What if she never got over Beau?

A knock at her door interrupted her thoughts and for one glorious, fanciful moment she imagined it was Beau on the other side of the door come to kidnap her and take her back home with him in a scenario straight from their video game.

But of course it wasn't Beau. She sat up tall, swiped the tears from her eyes with her fingers and cleared her throat. "Come in."

The door swung inward and General Dwight D. Sturgess strode into the room. As always, his steel-gray hair was clipped close to his head. He wore a starched white shirt and black linen slacks and his shoes were polished to a high sheen. His jaw was set, his eyes narrowed.

Marissa leaped to her feet and stood at attention beside her desk. "Good morning, sir."

"Your aunt tells me you got back two weeks ago and you didn't call me. Why not?"

The General came close, treading back and forth in front of her as if he were reviewing his troops. If he had a riding crop she had no doubt he would have been slapping it across his open palm.

"I've been busy."

"Too busy to call your father? That's no excuse."

"You're right, sir. My negligence is unacceptable."

Her father slowly glanced around the office. "So, you finally got your promotion."

"Yes, sir."

"And this office is the result?"

She nodded.

"Why isn't it a corner office?"

"Because only the president has a corner office."

"And why aren't you president?"

"Dad!"

"Marissa." He arched his eyebrow. "I raised you to be a winner. Why are you satisfied with crumbs?" He swept his hand at their surroundings.

"I've got a view of Central Park," she said, desperate to get him to see the promotion was a good thing. She stepped to the window and parted the blinds.

He walked over and peered out. "It's only a partial view."

"Well, yes."

He shook his head.

"What?"

"I'm disappointed."

"Disappointed?" She clenched her fists. "But I did what you've been pestering me to do for three years. I got that promotion. I'm the account director. My salary has almost doubled."

"Too little, too late. General Jenkins's daughter is two years younger than you and she's vice president of a pharmaceutical company, pulling down three hundred grand a year.''

Marissa's jaw dropped and she simply stared at her father as his words rang in her ears. Nothing she had ever done was good enough to please him and he was never going to change. No matter what she did, he would always set the bar higher and higher with no end in sight.

''Well, I'm sorry you're disappointed. I'm disappointed, too.''

''Good. You should be disappointed when you fall short of your potential. Imagine, being proud of this pathetic office. Look, the carpet is frayed in the corner.'' He clicked his tongue in disapproval.

Marissa drew in her breath. She knew it was time to set things right. ''Oh, I'm not disappointed in myself, General. I'm disappointed in you.''

He looked taken aback. ''In me? When have I ever let you down?''

Sadness filled her. He simply didn't get it and he never would. The stunning knowledge hit her low in the belly and stung with sharp intensity. But her discovery was also freeing. Once she recognized that her father would never value her for who she was and not for what she achieved, she could stop turning herself inside out to please him.

He was never going to change, but she could. She already had changed. So much. And it was all thanks to Beau. He was the one who'd shown her she was a worthwhile, precious human being worthy of love and respect simply because she existed.

"It's okay," she said. "The world isn't going to come to an end because you disappointed me and I disappointed you. We've both had unrealistic expectations about each other for years."

"What are you talking about?" he badgered in his gruff voice.

"You wanted me to be a boy. You wanted me to be in the military. You wanted me to conquer the world on your behalf. But I can't be and do those things. It's never going to happen. Just as I've got to realize that no matter how hard I try, no matter how far up the career ladder I climb, you are never going to give me the kind of unconditional love I've always longed for. You're never going to value me for simply being your daughter."

"I don't understand." The General glowered, completely clueless to what had been going on in her mind for the past twenty-six years. "Tell me, Marissa, exactly when did *I* disappoint *you?*"

"All the time, Daddy," she whispered. "All the time."

BEAU ROCKED in the chair on the back porch of Greenbrier Plantation and gazed out at the riverboat cruising down the Mississippi while Anna dozed at his feet. He should have felt relaxed, peaceful, connected to the earth where he'd been born, but he did not.

He felt tense, disturbed and disjointed. His hands were clenched around the rocker arms, his posture rigid. These days, he barely slept more than a couple of hours a night and he'd lost five pounds because food held no appeal. Two weeks had gone by since Marissa had returned to New York and with each passing day his nerves twisted tauter.

The woman was driving him crazy. He couldn't get her out of his head, no matter how many games of pool he played at the Lingo Lounge. Everywhere he went he saw her purposeful strut, smelled her intoxicating scent, heard her melodious voice, felt her soft caress, tasted her fragrant flavor.

Without her, he was bored and restless and unhappy. She'd ignited the spark in him that before her appearance in New Orleans had almost died away. Now the flame burned high. He was hungry for work, famished to design more video games but most of all he was starving for the stimulation of his challenging, hardheaded woman.

He craved Marissa and no other.

"How long are you going to sit here and mope?" Jenny's voice broke through his fidgety ruminations. She was standing at the back door. "Your gloominess is chasing off the guests."

He shrugged. "I'm not gloomy."

"Yeah, right."

"I'm not," he said, but his protest sounded feeble even to his own ears.

"I'd say it was way past time you got your lazy carcass off the porch and went after her."

"I don't know what you're talking about," Beau denied.

"Oh, shut up. Nobody's falling for your strong silent type routine. We all know you're in love with her and hey, for what it's worth, I'm pretty sure Marissa is in love with you, too.''

''I'm not in love with her,'' but even as he said it, he knew it wasn't true. He loved her as he'd never loved another and he was just terrified to admit it.

''What are you so afraid of?'' Jenny asked, echoing the thoughts circling in his head.

''I don't want to rock the boat,'' he said.

''You're indulging yourself, luxuriating in sweet stagnation,'' Jenny accused.

He stared at his little sister, taken aback by her vehemence.

''If you don't go after her, Beau, you'll regret it for the rest of your days and deep down inside, you know it.''

''Get real. We go together like marmalade and sardines.''

''Baloney!'' Jenny shoved open the screen door and marched out onto the porch, eyes blazing. ''Marissa is the best thing that has ever happened to you. She blew you out of your stable, comfy environment. Which was exactly what you needed, and you showed her how to connect with her inner self. I've never seen two people better suited for each other than you'all.''

''She ruins my peace of mind,'' Beau mumbled.

''She gets you involved,'' Jenny countered. ''Don't think I don't see your pattern. Beau, you're my brother and the salt of the earth and I love you dearly, but you've got to recognize how you're shooting yourself in the foot.''

"And how's that, little sister?" Jenny was starting to piss him off.

"In order to survive life with Francesca you detached from what you really wanted in favor of her wants and needs. You learned to not rock that proverbial boat. You immersed yourself in games, and while it served you well as a kid, as an adult, it's getting in your way."

"Oh yeah?" Why was he feeling both shaky and excited by Jenny's confrontation. Why did his blood suddenly strum with an energy he hadn't felt since Marissa went back to New York?

"Yeah. I can't stand watching you wallow in misery. Marissa isn't like your mother. She's not trying to manipulate you. Stop playing mind games with yourself, get your priorities straight and go after her, man."

Beau said nothing. He realized Jenny was right. He'd allowed his stubborn pride to get in the way of what he really wanted. He had acted like an insecure jerk when he'd refused to accept her apology. What a callous ass he'd been, making her feel bad about who she was. How he must have hurt her.

He'd been trying to make her over in carbon copy of himself. He'd thought he held all the answers. He'd believed that she would be happier if she slowed down and took things easy, if she left the city behind. He was wrong to try and change her. So very wrong.

He wanted her for who she was. A competitive, strong, decisive woman who knocked his socks off, both in bed and out of it.

The revelation this self-honesty brought was staggering, but the minute he accepted the truth about himself he felt as if a gigantic chunk of granite had been pried off his chest.

There was only one thing left for him to do.

MARISSA SAT on the floor of her closet in her cargo pants, chucking out shoes. She winged a pair of beige sling backs she'd bought in celebration of acing her first college exam into the suitcase lying open in the middle of her bedroom.

Next came a pair of melon-colored mules, representing her first debate-team win. Black Louis Vuitton boots, Marc Jacobs coral open-toed pumps, Christian Louboutin sinfully scarlet ankle straps. Valedictorian, Rhodes scholarship, magna cum laude. Her accomplishments and the shoes piled up.

When she'd filled one suitcase, she started on a second. The shoes whizzed through the air, landing with a soft whapping sound. Whiz, whap, whiz, whap, whiz, whap, until the closet was empty of shoes and Marissa's hands shook from the expenditure of excess adrenaline.

Since her showdown with her father that morning, she'd been building toward this decisive and irreversible action. The moment she faced herself and admitted how empty her life had become. The moment she realized that for the last twenty-six years she'd been denying her authentic self and living a lie.

And Beau had been the key. He'd unlocked her heart and opened her mind. He'd taught her how to take pleasure in her own existence. How to truly value herself. That day in the virtual-reality chamber when she'd seen how she could change if she wanted, Marissa had freaked out, unable at that point to accept the fact that her old image of herself no longer worked. She'd lashed out at him, but he'd met her halfway, holding up a figurative mirror and showing her just how much she meant to him.

She hadn't appreciated everything he'd done for her until now.

So she was going back to Louisiana and she was taking her shoes with her. In order to prove to him exactly how much she'd changed, she planned on chucking them one by one into the Mississippi River. She was going to show him that they couldn't allow their vulnerabilities to run their lives, couldn't let their insecurities keep them from loving each other.

Her heart soared with the thought of seeing him again. Beau, Beau, Beau.

No one had every captured her imagination, her mind and her heart the way he had.

Before Beau, she'd always been attracted to competitive go-getters with a high-energy style and impeccable work ethic. But through either fate or destiny or kismet, she found herself in love with a comfy, homey man who made her feel calm, accepted and understood.

He'd challenged her in ways she had never dreamed possible. He'd called to the little girl in her who'd never really had a childhood. He'd resurrected her lost sense of innocence and coaxed her imagina-

tion to new and exciting heights. He had shown her
how to love and he'd given her back to herself. She
couldn't wait to get to Louisiana and tell him what
she'd discovered.

The doorbell rang, short-circuiting her thoughts.

Marissa got up, dusting her palms against the back
pockets of her pants. She padded to the open window
and peered down to see a deliveryman on the front
stoop of her apartment building.

"Yes?" she called down to him.

"I have a delivery for Marissa Sturgess."

"I didn't order anything."

"It's from a Beau Thibbedeaux."

Her spirits soared to the ceiling. Beau had sent her
a gift?

"Come on up." She went to the front door and
buzzed the deliveryman in. She jerked the door open
when he knocked a few minutes later.

"Sign here." The guy held out a clipboard for her.

"Where's the package?" Marissa asked, signing
the clipboard.

"Hang on." The deliveryman pulled something
from out in the hallway and carried it into her apartment.

Her heart caught in her throat. It was the rocking
chair she and Beau had made love in with a big red
bow attached to the back. Tears filled her eyes and
her knees shook.

"Thank you," she whispered and tipped the guy.

"That's not all."

"No?"

The deliveryman stepped back into the hall. What else had Beau sent her? Her stomach squeezed in anticipation.

And then there he was, standing in the doorway. Her soul mate, her life partner, the man she loved with every fiber of her being.

He had come to her, just as she'd been packing to go to him. He'd more than met her halfway.

He was wearing a business suit and his thick dark hair had been cut short. His eyes sparkled a welcome and his lips were curled in his lazy grin. Her heart stuttered and she forgot to breathe.

Their gazes connected, locked. The warmth of his steady eyes filled her up. It was a look so hot and weighted with meaning she felt as if he'd actually reached out and touched her in a spot so secret she hadn't known it existed.

''Wh-what are you doing here, dressed like that?'' She swept a hand at his suit.

''What are you doing dressed like that?'' He nodded at her casual clothes.

''I was on my way to Louisiana,'' she said. ''I quit my job today.''

''I know. I stopped by your office.''

''You did?''

''Yes, and when I found out what you'd done, I told your boss he couldn't accept your resignation.''

''You did?''

''Yep, and then he offered me a job. I took it.''

''I don't understand.'' She stood there, wanting to

fling herself into his arms but feeling uncharacteristically shy about it.

Luckily, Beau took matters into his own hands. He kicked the door shut behind him, stalked across the room and swept her against his chest.

"Let's see if this will explain things."

He kissed her as he'd never kissed her before. He kissed her as if their very lives depended on it.

Marissa closed her eyes and melted into him. Clinging to his neck, she moaned low and throaty. He was her everything, she thought dreamily. The other half of her. For the first time she could recall, she felt utterly at peace.

His fingers deftly slipped a hand up underneath her T-shirt and eased her bra aside.

Her breasts swelled and her nipples bloomed at his caress. She opened her eyes and looked into his face to convince herself this wasn't a dream, that Beau was really here.

"It's me. I'm for real," he said, reading her thoughts.

"You're coming back to New York?"

"Yes."

"But I thought you hated it here."

"How could I hate the place where the most precious woman in the world lives?"

Her heart thumped beneath his hand. He buried his mouth against her neck and her pulse fluttered from the heat of his naughty tongue.

"I'm sorry, Beau," she whispered. "For hurting you."

"I'm sorry, too, Princess. You were right and I was wrong. I was hiding out. I did run away."

"No. You just chose a simpler life. I should have respected your choices, not made fun of them."

"My choices were too simple by far. Reconnecting with my family was a good thing but inertia kept me from progressing. You were the irresistible force who stirred this immovable object. Thank you, Marissa, for giving me back to myself."

He smelled of sweet basil and man, his skin toasty warm beneath her fingers. Her blood flowed feverishly through her veins. She wanted him so badly she couldn't stand herself. She wriggled out of her pants and shirt. Then she took his hand and guided him where she wanted him to go. When he found her slick, ready wetness, she hissed in her breath and bit down softly on his bottom lip.

"Take me now, babe," she pleaded. "I need you."

He lifted her into his arms. "Where's the bedroom?"

"It's a two-room apartment."

"Gotcha." He carried her into the other room and she felt as if she'd finally awakened from an endless sleep to discover her real life had finally begun.

He almost tripped over the suitcases mounded high with shoes. "What's all this?" he asked, carefully skirting the obstacles.

She told him about her plans to lob the shoes into the Mississippi.

"A bit drastic, don't you think?" he asked and laid her gently on the bed.

"I want to prove to you that I'm ready to let go of my need to succeed."

"Dear woman." He kissed the tip of her nose. "You don't have to give up your shoes to prove anything to me."

"Really?"

"Really. Now, where were we?"

Quickly, he dealt with his clothes, shucking off his jacket and shirt and dispatching his belt across the room. He unzipped his pants and she shimmied out of her bra and panties.

Dropping his trousers, he hauled her to the edge of the bed, separated her thighs and plunged into her, groaning as her slick heat enveloped him.

Marissa sucked in her breath at the swiftness of their impact. They were both so needy and greedy. Arching her back, she raised her pelvis up to greet his eager thrusts, urging him on.

Ah yes, this was what she'd missed. This thundering connection, this force far greater than herself. This unconditional love.

The power of their joining robbed her of all thought. She could do nothing but ride the wave of delicious pleasure, urging him on by clamping her legs around his hips and pulling him deeper inside her.

He picked up her frantic rhythm and she knew this first time would be quick and frenetic. Beau tried to control himself. Marissa saw the struggle contort his features as he fought to slow their lovemaking.

"Let go," she whispered and he gave up the battle. With a helpless groan, he plummeted into ecstasy.

His wanton sound, his forward propulsion ignited her climax. Shudder after shudder rippled through her body, lifting her to exalted heights. A keening wail ripped its way up through her throat and mingled with Beau's harsh noise. Their sounds echoed sexily around the room.

He collapsed onto the bed beside her, dragging her with him, until he lay flat on his back and she was straddling him. She sprawled against his chest and he wrapped his arms tightly around her.

"I love you, Marissa," he breathed, a heady catch in his voice.

She pressed her lips to the hollow of his throat. "I love you, too," she whispered.

They stayed locked together for a long time. Marissa realized she'd never felt so complete, so content, so whole.

"I'm sorry," he whispered. "For the way I acted in the alley. For not trusting you. For believing the worst."

"My bet with Dash was before I met you. I didn't mean to use you, Beau, and it kills me to think I hurt you. I'm so very sorry."

"Shh, we both made mistakes, but the important thing is, we know we've got something special here. Something worth fighting for."

"You, Beau Thibbedeaux, are amazing."

"Not half as amazing as you." Love for her shimmered in his eyes and she realized her own worth. It had nothing to do with her job or her abilities or how many shoes she owned. In Beau's eyes she recognized her authentic self. He saw past all the surface trappings and he loved her for who she really was deep inside.

She kissed him. Slow, soft and languid. There wasn't any hurry. They had all night. Hell, they had the rest of their lives.

"Marry me, Marissa. We can live part-time in New York, part-time in Louisiana. We can have the best of both worlds. Action when we want it, quiet when we need it. Say yes."

"Yes, Beau," she cried and kissed him harder, tears of joy streaming down her cheeks. "Yes, yes, yes."

He kissed her back until their lips were sore, and then he began to spin a sexy fantasy about a slow-moving Cajun boy and fast-paced New York woman.

And as he talked, Marissa clearly saw the truth.

Great sex wasn't just about mind-blowing orgasms and Fourth of July fireworks. It wasn't just about whimsy and play and lighthearted fun. It was about a love so rich and true that acceptance was guaranteed and compromise was not compromise at all, but the joy of joining two halves into a whole.

She felt Beau harden again inside her as he pressed his lips against her ear.

"Come," he murmured. "It'll be…as you like it."

0106/14

MILLS & BOON®

Live the emotion

Blaze™

CUTTING LOOSE by Kristin Hardy

Sex & the Supper Club

A makeover. A masked stranger. A master suite. When Trish Dawson's new look attracts the attention of a fellow party guest, she decides to cut loose and go for it. When the mask comes off, not to mention his clothes, actor Ty Ramsay is revealed. Will this be a one-night only performance?

HARD TO HANDLE by Jamie Denton

Lock & Key

Successful lawyer Mikki Correlli has worked hard to achieve the perfect life. When she attends a "lock and key" party, she hopes to have some sexy fun, no strings attached. What she doesn't expect is to run into Nolan Baylor – her ex-husband.

VIRTUALLY PERFECT by Samantha Hunter

Raine Covington has found the perfect lover – online. When Jack's sexy words fly across the computer screen, he can seduce her in a heartbeat. So why is she feeling unsatisfied? Once Raine and Jack meet face-to-face, both are surprised at the outcome…

BARED by Jill Shalvis

Emma Willis never expects to find herself wearing next to nothing and posing for a sexy calendar, but she can't refuse her twin sister's request for help. All Emma has to do is follow the photographer's instructions. Easier said than done once she catches sight of the sexy photographer Rafe Delacantro.

On sale 3rd February 2006

Available at WHSmith, Tesco, ASDA, Borders, Eason, Sainsbury's and most bookshops

www.millsandboon.co.uk

0106/05a

MILLS & BOON

Live the emotion

Millionaire's Mistress

In February 2006, By Request brings back three favourite romances by our bestselling Mills & Boon authors:

The Sicilian's Mistress by Lynne Graham
The Rich Man's Mistress by Cathy Williams
Marriage at His Convenience by Jacqueline Baird

Make sure you buy these passionate stories!

On sale 3rd February 2006

Available at WHSmith, Tesco, ASDA, Borders, Eason, Sainsbury's and most bookshops

www.millsandboon.co.uk

Live the emotion

0106/05b

Bewitched by the Boss

In February 2006, By Request brings back three favourite romances by our bestselling Mills & Boon authors:

The Boss's Virgin by Charlotte Lamb
The Corporate Wife by Leigh Michaels
The Boss's Secret Mistress by Alison Fraser

Make sure you buy these irresistible stories!

On sale 3rd February 2006

Available at WHSmith, Tesco, ASDA, Borders, Eason, Sainsbury's and most bookshops

www.millsandboon.co.uk

0206/14/LC04

MILLS & BOON®

Blaze™

LOCK & KEY

Unlock the possibilities...

When three women go to a lock-and-key
party to meet sexy singles, they never
expect to find their perfect matches...

Hard To Handle *by Jamie Denton*
February 2006

On the Loose *by Shannon Hollis*
March 2006

Slow Ride *by Carrie Alexander*
April 2006

Indulge in these three blazing hot stories!

Available at WHSmith, Tesco, ASDA, Borders, Eason,
Sainsbury's and most bookshops
www.millsandboon.co.uk

0206/108/MB013

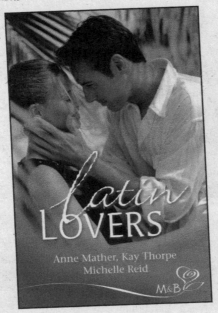

*Three fabulous stories from popular
authors Anne Mather, Kay Thorpe
and Michelle Reid bring you passion,
glamour and pulse-raising Latin
rhythm and fire.*

On sale 3rd February 2006

*Available at WH Smith, Tesco, ASDA, Borders, Eason, Sainsbury's
and all good paperback bookshops*

www.millsandboon.co.uk

0206/172/MB014a

BEFORE SUNRISE
by Diana Palmer

Enter a world of passion, intrigue and heartfelt emotion. As two friends delve deeper into a murder investigation they find themselves entangled in a web of conspiracy, deception...and a love more powerful than anything they've ever known.

THE BAY AT MIDNIGHT
by Diane Chamberlain

Her family's cottage on the New Jersey shore was a place of freedom and innocence for Julie Bauer – until tragedy struck...

Don't miss this special collection of original romance titles by bestselling authors.

Available at WH Smith, Tesco, ASDA, Borders, Eason, Sainsbury's and all good paperback bookshops

www.millsandboon.co.uk

LAKESIDE COTTAGE
by Susan Wiggs

Each summer Kate Livingston returns to her family's lakeside cottage, a place of simple living and happy times. But her quiet life is shaken up by the arrival of an intriguing new neighbour, JD Harris…

50 HARBOUR STREET
by Debbie Macomber

Welcome to the captivating world of Cedar Cove, the small waterfront town that's home to families, lovers and strangers whose day-to-day lives constantly and poignantly intersect.

Don't miss this special collection of original romance titles by bestselling authors.

Available at WH Smith, Tesco, ASDA, Borders, Eason, Sainsbury's and all good paperback bookshops

www.millsandboon.co.uk

2 FREE

BOOKS AND A SURPRISE GIFT!

We would like to take this opportunity to thank you for reading this Mills & Boon® book by offering you the chance to take TWO more specially selected titles from the Blaze™ series absolutely FREE! We're also making this offer to introduce you to the benefits of the Reader Service™—

- ★ **FREE home delivery**
- ★ **FREE gifts and competitions**
- ★ **FREE monthly Newsletter**
- ★ **Exclusive Reader Service offers**
- ★ **Books available before they're in the shops**

Accepting these FREE books and gift places you under no obligation to buy, you may cancel at any time, even after receiving your free shipment. Simply complete your details below and return the entire page to the address below. You don't even need a stamp!

YES! Please send me 2 free Blaze books and a surprise gift. I understand that unless you hear from me, I will receive 4 superb new titles every month for just £3.05 each, postage and packing free. I am under no obligation to purchase any books and may cancel my subscription at any time. The free books and gift will be mine to keep in any case.

K6ZED

Ms/Mrs/Miss/Mr ....Initials ....

BLOCK CAPITALS PLEASE

Surname ....

Address ....

....

....Postcode...

Send this whole page to:
UK: FREEPOST CN81, Croydon, CR9 3WZ

Offer valid in UK only and is not available to current Reader service subscribers to this series. Overseas and Eire please write for details. We reserve the right to refuse an application and applicants must be aged 18 years or over. Only one application per household. Terms and prices subject to change without notice. Offer expires 30th April 2006. As a result of this application, you may receive offers from Harlequin Mills & Boon and other carefully selected companies. If you would prefer not to share in this opportunity please write to The Data Manager, PO Box 676, Richmond, TW9 1WU.

Mills & Boon® is a registered trademark owned by Harlequin Mills & Boon Limited.
Blaze ™ is being used as a trademark. The Reader Service™ is being used as a trademark.

CAI
Rom1

We hope you enjoy this book. Please return or renew it by the due date.

You can renew it at www.norfolk.gov.uk/libraries or by using our free library app.

Otherwise you can phone 0344 800 8020 - please have your library card and PIN ready.

You can sign up for email reminders too.

NORFOLK ITEM

30129 088 520 003

NORFOLK COUNTY COUNCIL
LIBRARY AND INFORMATION SERVICE

Also by Laura Martin

The Brooding Earl's Proposition
Her Best Friend, the Duke
One Snowy Night with Lord Hauxton
The Captain's Impossible Match

Scandalous Australian Bachelors miniseries

Courting the Forbidden Debutante
Reunited with His Long-Lost Cinderella
Her Rags-to-Riches Christmas

The Ashburton Reunion miniseries

Flirting with His Forbidden Lady
Falling for His Practical Wife

Matchmade Marriages miniseries

The Marquess Meets His Match
A Pretend Match for the Viscount

Discover more at millsandboon.co.uk.